the
bride
stripped
bare

Editor: Calum Kerr
Typesetter: Victoria Hooper
Cover Photo: John Brewer
johnbrewerphotography.com

Dog Horn Publishing
6 Athlone Terrace
Armley
Leeds
LS12 1UA
United Kingdom
doghornpublishing.com

Previous publication history as follows:

Axis – Cherry Bleeds, 2008
Fly – Stranger Box, 2006
I know you – Flashing in the Gutters, 2006
Le café Curieux – Purple Verse, 2007 (as Le Café Rouge)
Solid Gold – Nemonymous 2005
Still Life – Cold Print 2003
Sweetmeats – Twisted Tongue, 2006
The Pleasure Principle – 3:AM 2007
The Suicide Room –Horror Express, 2004
This Is Not Kansas – Thieves Jargon, 2007
Will Travel – Dogmatika, Spring 2008

If you enjoyed this title, please share it with your friends.

The Bride Stripped Bare

INTRODUCTION:
RACHEL KENDALL STRIPPED BARE
by
Peter Tennant

I can't remember when I first became aware of Rachel Kendall.

Looking back it seems that she was always around, one of the neighbourhood girls, to subvert the title of a Suzanne Vega song, in the same way that I was one of the neighbourhood boys, the neighbourhood being the small press, or the independent press if you're a bit more uppity. It's a neighbourhood in which everybody knows everybody else without really knowing each other at all, if you get my drift. I have vague memories of reading some of Rachel's stories and reviews, and we'd even had work appear in the same places – *Dead Things, Darkness Rising, Strix* – shared a Table of Contents or two, an ersatz kind of intimacy.

I *can* remember though when we first had direct contact. It was the spring of 2006, and Rachel submitted an article, *Prague: A City of Ghosts,* to *Whispers of Wickedness,* a magazine for which I was then acting as non-fiction editor, and I was happy to accept it, as it was a classy piece of work. After that we corresponded a bit, discovering that we had a lot of shared interests – Henry Miller, surrealism, David Lynch, Tim Burton, fairy tales, pan fried erotica – and I had work published in the magazine Rachel edits, *Sein und Werden,* which is as eccentric and eclectic and idiosyncratic as she is. It was the start of what is conventionally called a beautiful friendship, a converging of agendas, or something like that, and along the way I started to pay more attention to her writing and fell in love with what this woman does with words.

So, skip forward to the present moment in time, and Rachel has a collection of stories out called *The Bride Stripped Bare*, and here I am writing the Introduction and wondering what the hell to say. Perhaps the first thing I should say is that you're probably not going to like everything in this collection.

Yeah, yeah, I know. I should be trying to sell you on *The Bride Stripped Bare*, but hey, if you're reading the Introduction then you've already bought the book, it's one of those done deals. And it's okay to not like every story in this collection, really it is. I'm writing the Introduction and I don't like every story, as for example "IIIVVWVVIIIVV". Shit, I don't even know what the title of that one means. This isn't a packet of chewing gum, with every stick the same shape and size and produced to a factory standard. If we need a produce metaphor, and it seems we do, then this book is a box of luxury chocolates, possibly made in Belgium or Switzerland, somewhere foreign and slightly exotic anyway, and fine and dandy as that is, it's a given that there's going to be an orange crème or two in the mix.

Anyway, with that disclaimer out of the way, let's talk about what you are going to like, about why Rachel Kendall is special, and why her work matters, and why I'm writing this Introduction.

Most of us in the small (or independent) press, we're just telling stories, and I don't intend to demean anyone by saying that, least of all myself, because telling stories is a pretty important thing. It's the way we thinking animals structure our world and make sense of things, and that's more true for writers than for anyone. Words are our tools, the building blocks with which we work to assemble something that will stand against the tempests of reader disbelief. We talk about themes and subtexts and emotional resonance and a thousand and one other things that make us seem intellectual as fuck, and all of it is true, every single word, but hey, when you get right down to it we're just telling stories.

Rachel Kendall is different.

Oh, she's just telling stories too, but this is one of those rare occasions when it's a secondary concern because I suspect for Rachel Kendall words are more than tools, building blocks, what have you. They're magical formulations, cantrips, spells, enchantments, alchemy to transfigure the base material of life into the pure gold of language. She writes prose with a poet's ear, and I honestly believe that, while most of us would diligently search out what we consider to be the right words, Rachel Kendall would prefer the most beautiful, the phrase that is the richest with lyricism and imagery, strangeness and charm. The miracle is that so often those distillations turn out not only to be the right words, but also the best words, so that reading her work one stumbles across a line or an image that flares up like a firework going off right in front of your face, something that will stay in the memory long after the story is done.

The essence of a moment.

But of course not all of those moments are such as to be conventionally beautiful. Kendall uses the most captivating language to describe terrible events, to lull the reader with her voice and then take him or her out of their comfort zone and challenge us to look at the most repellent of things. She has a fascination with the seamy underside of life, the spunk stains and shit streaks on bed linen in roach infested motel rooms, pus oozing from a festering wound and the mottled discolouration of bruised flesh, the body with its limbs twisted askew like a Hans Bellmer doll. Kendall takes these things and she finds glamour of a kind in them; she is a prurient writer, and she brings out that quality in us too, she gives us an itch that we just can't help but scratch. But she also knows how to cherish the broken things, the things that are discarded and reviled, caring about them every bit as much as she does the accoutrements of beauty, the orthodox signifiers of fascination we place in our art galleries and on the lids of our chocolate boxes, even those from Belgium and Switzerland. As a writer she embraces all of life, and turns her back on nothing except perhaps the ordinary.

And perhaps not even that.

There's pain here too, an honesty and rawness of emotion that gets under the reader's skin and insinuates itself into our being, so that we wince at the plight of a woman with post-natal depression who has sacrificed her baby, another who is faced with a terrible abortion, a third who comes to terms with her hunger for violent sex, a man who cannot connect with his humanity even through the act of murder. This is the freak show, make no mistake about it, and if Kendall's characters appear outwardly as normal as the rest of us, then be sure that inside they are every bit as deformed and grotesque as anything put on the screen by Tod Browning. Kendall gives us these painful truths, is more honest than most of us have the stomach for, but there's nothing gratuitous involved when she does so and she manages to avoid the judgemental, to find compassion and pity for the terrible deeds her characters commit, the people they become, to show us that it's only through fate and happenstance and blind luck that we don't do likewise.

Most of us are just telling stories. I see a familiar name in a Table of Contents or on the cover of a book, and I have a reasonable idea what to expect from them, but with Rachel Kendall I never have that feeling. I imagine her as a lady magician, playing to the crowd in spandex and fishnet tights (though I suspect she wouldn't be seen dead in such a get-up), and I don't have a clue what she'll do for her next trick, what she'll pull out of her silk top hat, if it will make me feel sick or give me a hard on, make me cry or punch the air in joy, whether it will be erotica or horror, mainstream or genre, linear narrative or experimental, intimately personal or speaking of the universal, or some confabulation of all those things.

The only thing I know for certain is that it will be magical, or the next best thing this tawdry world of cause and effect will allow, and I want to read whatever she commits to paper.

Kendall is a writer who pushes the envelope, who dares to take risks, to challenge herself and, to return to an earlier point, that is why you are probably not going to like all the stories in this collection. If you're a writer and you take risks, if you avoid the formulaic, then there are going to be moments when you fuck up, when you fall flat on your face. It goes with the territory, as all the hip kids say.

And that's my lot, so now go and read the stories, and do so knowing that there are going to be a lot that you *will* like, though perhaps like isn't quite the right word.

Rachel Kendall has a unique voice, a voice that echoes with all she has read and experienced, all life has taught her, and if she doesn't always tell us things that we want to hear, then that's just another reason why we need to listen.

CONTENTS

I Know You

Every hotel room is the same, its sterility as conducive to forgotten memories as the white scent of fresh linen. Totally devoid of character: not a single picture hangs on the magnolia walls. The wooden furniture is identical in each, the bedspreads of matching design. The lamps all have the same wrist-thin stems attaching them to the walls, a Gideon bible in the cabinet on the left side, even the stains on the mattresses could be identical.

This type of hotel doesn't attract tourists and holiday-makers. They're not situated on banks of pretty rivers or the sun-shimmering beaches of the South coast. These are one-night stays. Stop-overs. Perhaps a once-there and once-back. Business men. And their personal assistants. Might as well rent by the hour. I have every angle covered. My tracks are non-existent, my future as obvious to me as it is obscure to them. I have blind-sided them. I follow my route on the TV. I'm not stupid. I know they show only what they want the public to know. Still, it's good to know even that much.

I have ascetic intent. I will abandon all in a moment, god included. I can give up my desires if it should come to that. I need nothing. I am not a caryatid. I am not the backbone of the state. I *am* the state. But there are rules, many and unforgiving. Each must be adhered to, otherwise you could end up looking death or the devil in the face.

I have never picked someone up so close to the hotel. Usually I roam, I search. I am not an opportunist, I don't pick capriciously. I am not a carrion crow, feeding off the remnants of society's kill. I pick them ripe and plush and in their prime. I saw him, arrogant, sleazy, blond highlights in his hair, an expensive suit, and a cast on his leg. I offered my help in

1

such a way that made him feel superior. He was perfect. But the location, the hotel was not.

"I know you," he said when the door to my room clicked shut behind him. Had he been watching my progress? Following me? I wanted to deny everything. I wanted to admit it all. But by then it was too late for a threnody.

I woke up on the bed.

I am bridled. Hog-tied. Naked. My arms jutting out at odd angles, my back stinging with the scratches and tears of his belt buckle. On my front, my neck is sore with the strain of holding my head up to breathe, but the snot and tears and blood are thick in the back of my throat. My head throbs. I see his cast discarded on the floor, hear his breathing heavy and exhilarated. "I know you," he says, "you're just like all the rest."

51 weeks

We are members of something unique; a small collective, a thumb-sucking comfort. We are emotional refugees who fled the sanctimonious core of society, who seek to reconcile with the truest, most unconventional order.

We met on the internet, conferred electronically, planned telephonically and then gravitated to this one place, Pescara, Italy. A warehouse, hot with a vaguely meaty odour, plastic shards hanging like stalactites from a high ceiling.

The devil wears a sandy coloured suit. His flesh is tanned. The shades worn indoors and the sculpted beard betray his cool and his wealth. But there will be wealthier, more powerful demons above him. He is Tuvia. Tuvia is our guide.

There are twenty seven of us here. Some are people I have met before, some are new members. Some wear the expression of accismus, others' eyes dart nervously. We are teachers, officials, artists, and nurses, in blue and white collars. We are unemployed, unemployable, homeless, 'cured', bullies, bullied, pugilists and pacifists. And we have one thing in common – a need for satiety. Some of us have points on our license, criminal records for indecency, drug habits. Others own firearms, fucked up lungs, multiple piercings. And for us, nothing is ever enough.

Pescara is picture-perfect, a postcard paradise. Clear warm water, a blazing white sun, sandy beaches, coloured houses trailing flowers.

But we're all blinkered. We see only what we choose. Or, at least, only that which we're allowed to see. We sleep during the day and come nightfall we prepare to be shown our unHoly Grail.

I've been a member for four years. Once a year we all meet. It is our holiday and our reunion. For the other 51 weeks of the year we carry on as normal. We wait for the pubs to open so we can have that first drink of the day. We masturbate at the sight of lovers groping in the backs of cars. We steal the neighbour's kids' pet rabbit and saw off its ears before placing it carefully back in its hutch. We shoplift. We write letters to the editor. We have affairs and blackmail magistrates and lie on our tax returns.

What we want can be seen on a hundred different sites on the internet. But what we need is the chance to get involved. We want to submerge ourselves in the action, not sit alone in a room, staring at the monitor. Here is a group of like-mindeds to share the pleasure with. People we might meet in the flesh and start an actual friendship with. We help each other out, make suggestions, offer services, lend money, supply drugs. Hits and misses. I helped out a woman who went by the name of Rose (a woman by any other name. . .). She wanted to live out her rape fantasy. She lived a few hundred miles from me and I offered my services. We made plans. As she walked jauntily through the park near her four-bed, two-car home, I jumped her. I ripped and kicked and tore my way between her legs. Fucked her, pissed on her bloody face, kicked her a couple more times in the ribs and fled. It didn't fulfil any of my desires. I hoped it filled hers. I never heard from her again..

My first 'outing' with the group was in my home town of London. Tuvia led what was then only five members into the warm basement of an empty house with boarded-up windows and a pervasive smell of piss. Graffiti covered the walls inside and the toilet was clogged with shit. The squatters had to be forcibly removed before the body could be brought in. He'd been shot in the face; unidentified and possibly homeless, he'd been in the wrong place at the wrong time. Two of his fingers had been partially eaten away, by a stray dog, or maybe rats. His body had been cleaned up but his face was a mess. We were here to watch him decay. The heaters were there to speed up the process. The longer we were out here, the more money we had to part with.

So, we came and went as we liked for hours, days, weeks. One man vomited the first time he saw the body and didn't return. None of us spoke. We took our chairs or leant against the wall and performed our vigil around the corpse. We were not there to touch. We were eyes only. Eyes that widened further with every movement of flesh, every fluid and gassy ejection from every aperture. Our fingers merely held handkerchiefs over noses. Sometimes we went outside to breathe in the carbon monoxide from the day's mass of traffic. Going back inside was made harder by the fresh onslaught of decay. I found it easier to stay where I was. People brought me coffee and sandwiches, which I barely touched. I didn't want to miss a second of the show.

When Tuvia asked, I told. When he asked each of us in person and in private what effects the sight of the corpse had had on us, I told him none. I was disappointed, I said. I wanted more. It was all too passive, sitting and watching as nature did what nature does. It might make some people sick to the stomach, it might revolt others with its obvious mortality show, the reminder that this is how we will all end up. But what was it, really? It was nothing. It was a cycle. It was not enough.

I think Tuvia took note of my grumblings as the following year we ended up in Madrid at two in the morning, sitting behind glass on a second storey, watching a dog fight. Pit bulls. At least in part, these dogs had been bred to be fighting machines. Starved, beaten, kicked, they had been revved up like bulls before a fight. They ran at each other like they had been shot out of a cannon. I was impressed at first. The way their muscles rippled. The way their short legs pounded the floor. The way they tore at each other, ripping off a nose in one bite, taking out an eye, sinking teeth deep into the other's shoulder, through muscle, ripping off flesh till the bone was visible. Exhausted, they continued dripping blood, legs buckling, the chant of the men around them urging them on until one just gave up and the other tore its corpse to pieces.

"Why were we behind glass?" I demanded to know the next day.

I'd found the missing piece. Sitting on the edge of my chair, face inches from the clear obstacle, I'd been denied a right to be part of the action. I wanted to be down there where it happened. I wanted to be jostled by the crowd, smell the sweat of the men, be deafened by their shouts, wave money about, hiss and spit and clap the winner on the back.

"Too dangerous," was his answer. "These are very violent men. They know each other well. They've been face to face with each other for years. They don't take kindly to strangers. They're not here to put on a show for tourists."

"So give me something I can be part of," I spat at him. "It's what I pay you for. Give me something real, something I can touch and smell and feel."

The next outing was for me alone.

He took what I had said to heart and a few days later a black car pulled up outside my hotel room. I was alone at the time, drinking bourbon, lying on the bed staring at the stains on the ceiling. I wasn't prepared for three men to come knocking at my door, with guns and rope and heavily disguised voices.

When I woke I was back on my bed. Tuvia was sitting beside me. He cocked a brow when he saw me, shone a light into each of my eyes in turn. Perhaps for show, perhaps he was actually concerned. He nodded, satisfied.

"How do you feel?"

There was a question I couldn't answer in a flash. I felt. . . hungover. My head cracked and splintered, my eyes felt like they might roll out of their sockets. It was as though all the fluid in my body had been drained out. I was a pit of sand, and it felt like someone had been digging away inside me. Gradually I became aware of a pain in my genitals. What started off as a low throb and hum worked its way up to an acid burn as my foreskin began to peel off, followed by layer and layer of skin until I expected to find a bloody red stump in place of my cock. When Tuvia saw my pain he lifted the bed sheet (and here I discovered I was naked) revealing two metal spikes going in one side of my penis and out the other.

"Do you remember anything?"

I shook my head, closed my eyes, the pain almost visible to me. "Get them out," I said.

"Of course. But first, watch."

He pointed a remote control at the TV at the end of the bed and I watched myself in grainy black and white. The whole thing had been filmed, from my kidnap, to the S&M club, to the loss of my body in a mass of flesh, to the woman (man?) towering over me, my body on a rack, my penis limp, and the insertion of the spikes into my flesh. My face did not even register pain. Had they filled me so full of drugs I was completely numb? Blood, thick and black on film, covered my legs. They left me there, carried on cavorting around me. The screen faded to black.

The offending articles were removed from my cock and though it hurt to piss for a few weeks and sex was completely out of the question, there was no lasting damage. These people were not amateurs. Still, in the end, I had to ask Tuvia what was the point?

"You didn't like it?"

"There were many things I didn't like about it. I wanted action and you offered me a passive role again. Not only that but I was drugged beyond awareness. I felt nothing. I saw nothing. I asked you for something, Tuvia. Give me something."

And now, a year later, in a warehouse in Pescara, we wait for the devil to speak.

What he offers for our amusement has me turning on my heel and heading for the door.

"Mike," he shouts after me. "I need to talk to you after the meet."

I nod and head outside, lean against the wall to smoke a cigarette.

Watching people fight to the death. Men, high on angel dust and god knows what else, ripping at each other like animals. I've seen it all before. Here he is, suggesting a spectator sport yet again. Crude, yes. Dangerous and vile, of course. But passive all the same. After watching the dogs, I'd wanted to be a part of the crowd. But now I knew it still wouldn't be enough.

"I want to fight," I say when he comes out of the warehouse. "I want to get my hands dirty this time."

He shakes his head.

"I will not have your death on my hands. Nor any death from this collective. You know that. If you want to commit suicide, you do it on your own."

I shake my head in return. "I can win."

"No, you can't."

And then he takes my hand. "Come," he says. "I promise you will not be disappointed."

When I was a kid, a boy of twelve or thirteen, me and Gareth used to watch Mrs P undress at night. Peeping through the corner of the window where the net didn't quite meet the edge of the frame, we'd take it in turns to watch the luminous flesh slowly appear as clothes were shed. She always slept naked and always went to bed at least an hour before her husband. We'd get a full view of her bush, that beautiful mound of thick black hair, her wide hips and thighs. I would watch the way Gareth's mouth tightened when he was aroused, and his neck would get blotchy. Later we would shoplift from Smiths and play chicken with the cars on the main road. Always looking to get our kicks. He was killed in a simple automobile accident. A drunk driver rammed into the back of his parents' car, killing him and his dad outright. After that I started to steal into people's houses at night and take any crap I could carry in two hands. But without my look-out, my ally, I was no good and landed myself in jail more than once. Sitting alone in the cell I would think of Gareth. How he had been cheated in death. It had crept up on him and then taken him in one ear-splitting moment, by a drunken man, a regular, normal human being, soused, not even in control. A totally passive death.

The men have weapons. I thought they would be fighting bare-fisted but no, they both have metal scaffolding poles to fight with. They charge each other, weapons held high. One knock to the skull would be enough, but we want the fight to last awhile. So they aim low, shattering kneecaps, breaking ribs. There is quite a crowd here, and we are in amongst them this time, close enough to be hit by an occasional splatter of blood. We shout and jeer, clap and yell 'hit him hit him hit him'. The smaller man bites off a large piece of his tongue as metal crashes into the side of his head. He spits it out and grabs the other man in a half-nelson. They hold back a little more than the dogs, though they growl and wheeze and bark at each other. One is on his knees, vomiting, and the other takes the opportunity to kick him in the ribs. They don't hate each other. They probably don't even know why they're doing this. The survival instinct is as strong in these men as in any other animal. That is all. Kill or be killed. I can feel the pulse of the crowd. I have a semi-erection. Not far from where I stand, a man is masturbating furiously, eyes locked on the fight. We want a victory. For many of the people here, it's simply a business transaction: winner takes all. For the rest of us, we don't care who takes the crown. All we want is to witness a triumph.

It ends with a crescendo. Back from the brink, the smaller of the two men wins the war with an attack of blows to the head. The tall man is left with no face, his head mashed to a bloody pulp, his body black and blue. After much waving of money and pats on the back, the crowd begin to disperse, some happy with their winnings while others, dejected, return to the fringe they came from. Some stragglers wait behind. I wait for Tuvia, who is talking to a big man wearing tattoos and a holster. When they walk over to me I unfold my arms and stare hard into the man's steel-grey eyes. With a nod from Tuvia, he hands me the gun. I am blank-faced and blood-smeared. But he has seen something in me.

"Kill him," Tuvia says, pointing to the winner of the fight who sits on the floor sucking on the bloody end of dog-eared cigarette.

"But he won the fight."

9

"The rules of the game Mike. The winner must die as well as the loser."

"But—"

"No, Mike. If you can't do it, it's fine."

The tattooed man is getting impatient. I look down at the target. He is watching me, my face. Does he look smug, or is it my imagination? Does he *want* me to kill him? Is he daring me? I point the gun at his head and pull the trigger.

"So," says Tuvia as we walk away from the murder scene. "Did you feel something then?"

"No," I say. "I didn't feel a thing."

Blood Money

I was feared. By many. By people of a certain ilk. Those scabby low-down individuals who are always in trouble. Financial, legal, and moral. They're pursued by it, sometimes from birth. Abandoned, kept by the state, fostered over and over by kind people they spit on because they don't know how to show their gratitude. Drug taking, drug dealing, borrowing, stealing, killing, never the boss, always answering to someone higher up, someone like me. I was the bogeyman. I was the needling bride. I was the one hiding under the bed with maggoty eyes and a swivelling head.

I have a boss of my own, of course. Who is at the top of the pyramid? It certainly isn't me, though I am higher up than most. I still have to answer to those on the next level. And at the very top? The one we all answer to? It's still money, or god, depending on your faith. I do this for money just the same as those I kill.

There are simple rules. There will always be rules. Rules are needed for stability, for a working business, environment, economy and society. Those who break the rules will be punished. Crime does not pay. Except when it does. But payment is high: sometimes it's a life, sometimes it's nothing more than a small vial of blood. It depends on the debt.

My name has been whispered around vicious circles for many years now. I have become the best, the most feared, envied, a schoolboy fantasy. Those who are not capable of criminal deeds sketch me into their notebooks and their dreams, hear my footfalls as I stride toward them all black leather and impossible statistics. A waist they'd love to wrap their fingers around and breasts to suffocate them. I am not a reality for them. I am merely a comic book villain. To the others, the ones who pay my bills, I am all too real, and although there are a select few who have nothing left but the fantasy of the blood girl's needle as their last memory, in most I instil the kind of fear that prevents, as well as punishes, crime.

It is inevitable that in a business like mine, you will reach the point where you think you have seen everything. I thought so. Admittedly I thought so a few times. It started when I was young, the first time I paid a visit to a client under the age of eighteen. Of course age does not bend the rules in this game, but I was still a little shocked, one might even say distressed, that first time. Then there was the first AIDS victim, paying for a crime he had committed many years earlier, when he was still well enough to flee. He begged me to take all of his blood. But I took only what I had been instructed to take, and left him unconscious.

It is surprising how many will beg to be killed, drained completely, as though I was an angel of mercy. There are those with wives and jobs, those you catch in bed with another who hold out their arms, exposing their blue veins: *take what you need, just don't tell my wife.* And then there are single mothers with babies in their arms and wide-eyed children watching in fear as their mother is held down, her skin turning blue and then black in the pincers' grip, and her face turning white, whiter, whitest as she slumps to the floor, sometimes never to regain consciousness. I slide the needle back into its silver container, strip off my gloves and stride away with the cold-box of blood. To deliver, and to await my next order.

How could I have known the world could stop turning as simply as that? That in a moment, such a small measure of change could take place, a rolling snowball of the end of all this? Of me? One minute I was running ahead, ambitious, materialistic, feared, the best. The next, I had become practically one of them.

The moment of change is a pinpoint. I know it exactly. I have wished, dreamed, of going back and changing my history but alas, it can never happen. That day, that girl, that moment of. . . what was it? A memory. I saw something in her eyes, I could have been looking in a mirror. She was 14 at most, sitting in that leather armchair whose innards spilled from several holes and slits. Looking small, like Alice in

12

Wonderland, small and bruised, yellowing arms held out to me. In the background the mother's wailing distracted me. Wringing bird hands, her small skeleton in the doorframe overshadowed by her brutish husband and his fat mallet-like hands. It was obvious, alas, and happened too often, that deals were made. Young blood has always been worth more and if they can get it and others can be let off for it, the deal is set. All too often a child's blood paid for a parent's misdeeds and this, this one thing, affected me time and time again. To the point where I now began to falter. I was only doing my job, mellifluous as it usually was. I was the good guy, generally. And I was respected. But where was the respect in this? This was cowardice, and this was me following the rules when the rules had begun to shift like tectonic plates, and crash against each other. She said nothing, the girl, when I turned away and walked back to the door. I could hear the father's footsteps and then he crashed open the door and was all fists and threats but a knife to his throat stemmed the flow and when I threatened to cut off his balls and let him bleed to death if he ever used his daughter in this way again, I could see in his eyes that my reputation was still intact.

I had a choice. I could return empty handed, or I could find a replacement. There are plenty of bums, drunks, homeless people who wouldn't put up much of a fight. But, chances are, they would be contaminated. I needed clean, pure, 5 star, red stuff. The father had the same blood type, but as it was his heroin addiction that had got him into this mess in the first place, he was hardly a good substitute.

If I were assigned the case then payment was blood. But it could just as well be a thumb, a leg, a kidney, or something less painful, more subtle, but just as damaging in the long run. It all depended which sector of the business lent the money in the first place. Payment could be health, wealth, sanity, sight, mental ability. Contracts were signed, nobody borrowed money blind. All clients were aware from the outset of the type of re-payment required if money was not an option. Always desperate to sign, confident of getting the money back to us, but all too often all spent up at the final count. A chemical injection here, a dip into a bank balance there, and a slow spiral into poverty, sickness or insanity, a total void, a vegetative state awaited them around the next bend. We don't play god. We don't hit out at random. We merely mete out the punishment.

In the end it was blindingly obvious. And easy. The answer was at my fingertips, and in my arms, my veins. I thought it over for maybe ten minutes. With every tick of the clock the little girl's blank stare moved further and further away, the scars in her arms that belied the number of times she'd actually sacrificed her blood for her father in other ways. I admit that my hands, usually so steady, were shaking as I uncapped the silver pen-shaped instrument that held the needle. I rolled up my sleeve and, using the tie from my bathrobe, I made a tourniquet and slipped in the needle. When I stick it into the arm of a client it slides in as though through soft cheese. The only resistance comes from the person themselves as they thrash against the cuffs which hold them down. But the skin itself almost opens itself up to the point. Piercing myself though, that first time, was very different. Almost as though the flesh itself were hardening its layers to push the needle back out. Funny how the mind plays tricks.

I still work for the business, but I no longer collect and deliver. I've been demoted. Now I am a barely-glorified secretary, taking the calls, arranging meetings, organising schedules. My reputation is not even dirty, it just isn't there. I have no reputation any more to speak of. There are others now, sturdier, thicker-skinned, hardened, who will take and take and take without a second thought. I have never been questioned. I guess they just saw it— the light fading, the skin losing its glow, my fainting spells. I always took care not to let the scars show, the bruises and lesions from skin forced between pincers (I left behind the comfort of the soft-towelled belt long ago), the holes, pin pricks, that crawled up my arms and my thighs and my stomach. When it was getting too difficult to sit down because of the puncture marks in my arse and groin, I moved to my hands and feet. So, the evidence is all there now, like a tattoo. At least my colleagues have the decency not to question me. They just avert their eyes, so I don't see their distaste, and hasten on. Soldier ants, just doing as they're told. I should stop, I know, before it kills me.

Eat Me, Eat Me

The shrivelled branches grasped the hem of Sarah's white skirt like witch's fingers as she skipped past them, and sighed with discontent when the material tore. Leaving a scrap of white in their fingers she moved away, singing, hand in clammy hand with the boy.

He was here on a promise. She was going to show him hers. Then he could go back to the others with a full account of the texture, curve, scent and, he hoped, the taste of the girl's cunt. Glass-footed she was, with one eye forged from metal, a hapless, pathetic thing who hip-hopped around, bungled and fumbled and not-so-nimbled her way into their chorus chants of obscenities. His friends didn't know he'd been in this precarious position before, waiting for deliverance, that he hung on her every promise with bated breath. Nobody liked her. She remained an enigma to some, a plaything to others. And soon, a mass of moist adjectives to Thomas and his pals. If he found himself lucky. She *had* seemed quite up for a bit of hanky-panky. In fact, it had been her suggestion they go into the woods at the back of her grandmother's house for a bit of in out in out.

Thomas didn't much like the old hag's house. It smelled rancid, and everywhere pots boiled strange brews; bottles containing murky liquids sometimes seem to shift of their own accord high up on a shelf out of reach; any number of peculiar insects were marching up and down the stairs at all hours of the day, and there were what looked like mouse droppings in the corners of every room. But at the back of the house was the forest. Practically the old woman's back garden. He'd never seen her in there though. Neither had he seen the girl, dancing naked in the moonlight, as the story went. And he'd been there often enough, camped out through the night, high on insecticide and a certain joie de vivre at someone else's expense. Usually this was his mother's, who hadn't yet noticed her depleting money stash, buried as it was beneath the fourteen mattresses on her orthopaedic bed.

"Did you hear that?" The high of his lascivious promise had begun to dwindle as soon as dusk grazed the uppermost branches of the dark green canopy. He wouldn't have shown fear, and had never before *felt* fear with the lads, even when they'd lain around a fire in the pinched darkness of a November night in a clearing they'd called their own. No. He only felt the fear with her.

She shrugged. "I heard an animal foraging or a leaf falling or a twig snapping or. . ." she pranced, tiptoes of tiptoes up to him, fingers clawed. "Maybe it was a beast. A wild animal come to rip us to shreds." And then she laughed the laugh that had earned her the title of witch.

"Don't be daft," he said. "This is England. The most we're going to see is a stray badger."

"Hm-hmm."

She took him deeper, deeper into the woods, to a place he'd never seen. He didn't realize he'd only ever been on the very periphery before. Here was darkness like he'd never imagined. A darkness that penetrated to his marrow, that made his heart pound against his chest. So when the wolf approached he didn't see it. He only sensed a change, a quick inhalation from Sarah, the hairs on the back of his neck rising. And then, then, that terrifying howl by his side that had the piss running down his trousers and his legs trying to buckle before he regained control and ran.

The wolf trotted over to Sarah like a trained dog. She stood stiff, barely daring to breathe, back pressed against the bark of an ancient gnarly tree. The animal's snout was long, its eyes yellow. It looked at her, sniffed at her, making no sound except for the short sharp inhalations of her scent, its damp nose pressed into her groin. And then it turned and ran. Following the trail of piss and fear.

* * *

The cold had begun to bite by the time the wolf came back. She heard the padding of its paws, the rush of undergrowth, and she heard its whispers. It called her name, as always. There was blood caked around its snout, its whiskers beaded. The scent was strong, red. She watched as its pink tongue curled out to smooth down the wet fur above its mouth. It seemed to grin at her.

"Come on, my girl," it said.

She began to back away, stumbling, one fleshy foot feeling what the other foot couldn't. Tripping backwards over thick tree roots and brittle branches that tried to raise the hem of her skirt, tried to pick their way inside underwear, pinching her nipples, scratching her face and tugging on her hair. She turned and ran in the direction of grandmother's house.

She stayed one beat ahead the whole time. She seemed to be running for hours, darting, stretching, kicking, skidding on golden fallen leaves, until she saw the back door and heard his blood-curdling howl. She ran into the house, closing the door behind her, but not fast enough as the wolf was in, sliding through the gap, too quick for a small human girl. He bounded onto the settee, leaving muddy footprints, he skidded along the smooth wooden floor and BAM. There was grandma with a rolling pin in her hand. She'd hit the wolf on the snout, hard enough to hurt but not hard enough to knock him unconscious. In fact, all she'd done was annoy him. In one leap he was on her, tearing at sagging flesh and brittle bones and dried up fingers and toes till there was nothing left but a heap of grandmother in a pool of blood.

Sarah watched it all from behind her hands, she gasped and swooned and almost fainted at the sight.

"Bad bad bad bad bad bad wolf," she said. "You ate Grandmother."

But the wolf looked so forlorn, so sad and pathetic. "I got a little carried away," it said.

"Oh, come here, you," she said, and rubbed the wolf's head between his eyes. "How could I ever stay mad at you, huh?"

He nuzzled into her breasts and she bowed her head to suck the blood from his whiskers. And then, with a glint in her good eye and the charm of a smile around her blood-smeared lips, she patted her behind and waltzed into the bedroom. The wolf followed her, that grin, those eyes, those large teeth and damp nose to taste the sourness of the old lady's bedroom, the doilies and the false teeth and china figurines. The wolf knew prey from this. She was never prey. She was always plaything. And as she knelt on the bed and raised her naked rump to him, he mounted her slowly, pawing her smooth naked back, and knew, as ever, that he had found his other.

This is Not Kansas

A pound of flesh in front and the middle finger of my reflection says 'I know this is horse shit' in two syllables. 'Pregnant' or 'baby'. Or 'floozy'—a word my grandmother might have christened me. I am a landscape. I am damp, stretched over rivers and valleys in this seventh month, stepping into the third tri, my belly the only evidence of an import. The girl in the mirror is sixteen, still pert, swollen, elastic and taut. In truth, I feel older. I am growing outwards. Did I even stop growing upwards yet?

Beside the mirror, next to the window, a clock to record the hours of payment and two calendars. One of them shows a wintry November scene, 1976. The other is open to January '77. The twelfth is circled in bright red, the date of the birth.

I hear the rumbling of tyres and look out of a window blinkered by red drapes. 'Royal red' Lotte calls it. All the rooms are decked out like this – red and gold sex, plump cushions and four-poster beds. She says these men pay by the hour for us to make them feel like kings.

I see Larry pull up in the van. When he gets out he instinctively looks up at the window. We look at one another and smile. I am the first to move away. I think he is hot for me. I like him too, especially in that blue polo neck jumper. He thinks he's Lou Reed, but that's okay. Lou Reed is cool. Today, while he makes his deliveries I watch as two women approach. It's only eight o'clock but wintry dark. The wind creaks around the house and the sign outside sings to and fro. I like the sign. Not the 'Greysylph Skies' in gothic lettering but the added red graffiti beneath – THIS IS NOT KANSAS. It's true we're not in Kansas anymore Toto, but then I didn't feel much at home in the last place either. At least here the flesh is willing.

One of the women carries a bundle clutched to her breast. The other, older one, folds her arms around nothing to compensate, or just to keep out the cold. I watch as the women step over a wooden sign on the floor, abandoned from the last of the protesters who left before the darkness and the ghosts of the house could swallow them. I can't read it from here but can guess what it says – 'Baby killers' or something just as subtle. Harsh words but it's an invisible battle. Rumours spread fast, even out here. They stick fast in the throat but once they're out they spread like fire. Word is that this is the hell mouth. Babies are supposedly made on the first floor and aborted on the second. Not true. I've even heard them say the buckets of blood, the red mesh flesh of the foetus birth is thrown from the windows for the wild dogs to devour.

The women have gone round the back. I wait for them to reappear minutes later, empty-handed as always, hair flying trinkets in the wind, faces cold, lips tight, no words to say but clocking up so many mute questions. I watch as they climb into a dark Allegro, drive away upstream in a silver cocoon, opposing the River Colne that carries mercury blood far from here. So they say.

I roll on black stockings: hold-ups as my suspender belt no longer fits. They are ripped to shreds, my contribution to the fantastic new punk scene hitting the streets. This and the black polish on my nails is as much as Lotte will allow. I tried for a studded dog collar but she said it would put the clients off, that they paid for girls, not anarchists.

I didn't tell Lotte at first. I was so desperate for money I didn't know what else to do. I planned to work here for a few weeks, just to sort myself out. And then one night she came up silently behind me, slid marbled hands around my belly and began to caress it. I felt her breath in my ear, her dyed black hair tickling my neck, and a whisper, "Are you pregnant, sweetie?" And after a three times denial her smile drew out the truth. But I don't know how she knew, because I wasn't showing. If anything, I was underweight, skinny and ribby. Women's intuition? Had she noticed I hadn't bled? She squeezed me so tightly I thought I would give birth there and then and she told me what a treasure I was. Then she told me why and for the first time in a long time I felt proud. She's like the mum every little girl dreams of.

It is a little before nine. I make my way downstairs to await the night's carnival.

"Hi, Eva. Hi, June."

I smile at the girls and they smile back. Heads nod, plumes of smoke emerge from crimson mouths. There are fifteen of us here. Most are now lounging on chairs, playing cards, dancing to The Pretenders, smoking, cursing, chatting. They are rounded, Amazonian, slim, athletic, panther-like, kittenish, anorexic, curvaceous. Some beautiful, others not. These are the girls who needed somewhere to run to, who were caught, or caught out; girls from Russia, one from Poland, five are Vietnamese. Girls between sixteen and thirty five, all with swollen bellies. Lotte, who doesn't tend to sit with us, is in her sixties. Too old to play; she's had her time. Together we laugh, we wait. I light a Marlboro and keep an eye on the door. Above us, high on the wall, a tiger prowls in the confines of an artist's brush strokes. Eva says it makes the place look more like an Indian restaurant than a whore house. But I like it, the power in its legs, the might of its open jaws.

The door swings open. It is only Larry. He looks nervous.

"Hi," he says to me, with a wave of his hand. No one else is privilege to this acknowledgement and I feel a little superior. He disappears into another room, hollowed out and confessional behind a pair of curtains we are never allowed to part.

There is a loud bang from behind the curtain. We look at one another. Lotte storms out, pencilled eyebrows fierce. Larry follows, lap-dog willing.

"Larry," I hiss. He comes over. The girls pretend to busy themselves with not listening. Lotte storms outside.

"What's going on?"

Nervously, fingers plucking at his gold-speckled beard, he looks around, then fixes his gaze on me. He stares at my eyes as though to let his guard down would mean to let his eyes wander all over my body. It gives me a thrill.

"There's been an accident," he says. "Joe smashed the van into a tree. He's okay; he's on his way now to Devon till it blows over. But the consignment is. . . The back doors of the van flew open and most of it was lost. The rest were pretty broken, probably all dead now."

"You mean he didn't stay? He didn't even check on them?" I feel sick.

"He wasn't going to stick around when the police turned up wanting to know why there were thirty dead babies scattered around a tree like bloody Christmas presents."

Thirty?

"I thought. . ."

I decide not to finish what I was about to say. Not now. But I thought they took a couple at a time. To Moscow, to Vasaa, to Madrid, to Sofia, to anywhere the babies were needed.

"Shit," says Maria. The girls are crowded round now, anxious, the babies inside them kicking in sympathy.

"What about Lebovitch?" I ask.

"He doesn't know yet. But when he does. . ." He nods to finish off the sentence. I understand.

"What'll happen?"

He shrugs and Lotte enters. We all shrink back, waiting for an explosion. Larry smoothes his trousers, looks at his feet. One lace trailing.

"I'm sure you've all heard," she says, one hand on the wide hip of her corseted hourglass figure. "Whatever happens, we carry on as normal. Okay? There are thirteen pregnant girls here. There is a constant supply of unwanted babies out there. This is a set back, but I will talk to Lebovitch and he will sort things out. Okay? And one more thing. Appointments only, ladies. No more drop-ins. We don't want the police sniffing their filthy snouts around here, do we?"

She points at me. "I have one for you." He must have asked for a young one, I think. Shit, this is the last thing I want right now. Visions of limbs, trunks like insect thoraxes, blooded heads, tiny hands, nails, toes. I have to look up to stop tears falling from my eyes. Larry watches me sadly as I go out the door. Sometimes I feel that he wishes he could 'rescue' me.

Fool.

I lead my client up the stairs; close behind me his hands on my hips. The first thing he notices is my bump. The first thing I notice is his, in his too-tight trousers.

"Can you still do it like that?" he asks, pointing to my heavy flesh as I shut the door behind him.

"Oh yeah, it won't hurt the baby."

But it's not the baby he's worried about. "I didn't pay to get crushed. I paid for a school girl."

"School girls get pregnant too, you know." I say it under my breath. I hate him; he has no respect. I wonder how many children he's spawned, but keep these thoughts to myself as I slip on a white shirt and struggle with a tie. He has stripped to his Y-fronts before I have stepped into the grey pleated skirt. Damn thing doesn't fit. I can't even pull it up to where my waist used to be. It's been a while since anyone asked for the schoolgirl thing. He is stretched out on the bed, waiting. Forget the skirt, he'll be too busy to notice anyway. I dab some perfume between my breasts and stride over him.

That's when it hits me. The pain. A great heaving pain that locks me inside myself and makes me double over. My client jumps out from under me. I remember that much. He runs faster than Roadrunner, grabs his clothes and is down the stairs screaming blue murder and I am doubled up on the floor, clutching at myself, thinking this is the worst pain I ever felt.

The room is white.

I am in a white room.

Is it heaven or hell or somewhere else?

The woman beside me might be my mother. She is squeezing my hand and reading a magazine she has laid out on the blue sheets which cover my stomach. She is looking down. She doesn't know I'm awake. I guess I make a sound because she looks up then and it's Lotte, and she strokes my chin and says, "How do you feel?"

I am wearing some kind of gown with a label that itches my neck. I feel sore. This is a single bed in a single room, with double doors at one end and double doors at the other. Somebody comes in through one set of doors and the leaves that sweep in with him show me the outside world.

"How is she?" It's a man. It's Larry. I smile when I remember and everything feels all right.

"I'm fine," I say, and he takes my other hand and squeezes it.

"It was hit and miss there for a while," says Lotte.

"Am I going to be okay?"

"Not you, the baby." Oh yes, the baby.

"Is it. . .?"

"It's a boy."

Again I feel tears in my eyes, a lump inside; not a living body but an emotion I haven't felt before. My hard shell is broken, my attitude shed like the leaves from the trees outside. I am maternal after all.

"Will he be okay? Will he be looked after? Will there be a couple waiting somewhere to take him and love him and. . ." I can hear myself getting hysterical and Lotte is hushing me, calming me.

"He's on his way now, to a couple in the Ukraine. He'll be loved, don't you worry."

I am not listening now. I can hear voices, bass, underwater, muffled, coming from the other side of the other doors. But before I can ask or say anything, Lotte has risen, "I'll be back to check on you later." She kisses me on the cheek and then she and Larry are gone.

I close my eyes. I can get through this. It's just the hormones. I've read books. It'll pass eventually. The voices are louder, shouting. I can't sleep. Two men, speaking in tongues. Vipers. They may be Russian. And then it stops. A door slams. Silence. And curiosity gets the better of me.

The doors swing open at a touch and I glide into the darkness, edging against the wall, like they do on TV; like they do in films. I am small, though my flesh feels too big. I am quiet. I know I shouldn't be here. I just want to know what the shouting was about; what I have missed. My fingers find the light switch and I illuminate the room.

What I see will give me nightmares for a long time to come. Until the sense is talked into me, until I become numb like the rest. What I see shocks me in that instant, so I fall to my knees and begin to sob. What I see is row upon row of incubators, a lab, a surgery. Eleven sets of eyes blink open at the white light disturbance. And twelve mouths open to cry; except that I don't hear a single sound from inside those tiny glass boxes. I hear only a gasp, emitted from myself as my hand goes up to my mouth.

I lift myself up, two hands on the wall, and move my heavy feet, take steps towards the babies and I think, 'is mine here?' Is he really on his way to some poor, barren couple with a ready-made nursery? Or is he here, with these other poor souls in this purgatory. I spot an incubator separate from the rest, far out in the corner under bright lights, and I know he is mine.

Walking between the beds, uncovered babies writhing pink worms with tiny arms and legs and. . . appendages. I dare myself to look closely into one, a brown baby, a mass of black hair on his head, and from his body, just above the clipped umbilical, I see another head, a squashed face on the front, wiry black hair on top, a neck, shoulders, one arm, rib-cage. . . all protruding from his, or her, brother. Its eyes are closed, gooey liquid around the lids, a frown above, its nose hardly there and dark lips open to a pink mouth just enough to let the air squeeze through.

I back up. There is a smell of something clean, sterilised, baby talc and iodine, bandages; and beneath it all, fresh wounds, old putrefactions and a green kind of coppery smell that clings to my throat. Lining the walls

26

are typical surgery implements, heart monitors, drips, tools to measure this and machines to regulate that. I sidestep to the next crib.

No, its head is enormous. Its egg yolk body too small for this huge head attached by a thread of a neck. The baby in the next has sewn up eyes, black cotton like long eyelashes joins top eyelids to bottom. Her mouth is open, she breathes peacefully. In the next I can hardly see the baby mass for the equipment around it, droning and pulsating, as though this baby is part human, part machine. I am going over to my boy, slowly, half wanting to cover my eyes. He is tiny, jaundiced and tiny, with tubes going up two nostrils the size of poppy seeds and a square plaster in the crook of each elbow. 'What have they done to you?' I think, and I begin to pound on the glass. He wakens, he doesn't see me, only begins to scream. And his cries can be heard, not like the others. He screams and he screams and then the door opens and two men come dashing in.

September 1977. I am painting Venka's nails a bright post box red. Larry is in the kitchen making us coffee. We are kind of 'together' now. It was inevitable. Maybe we'll get married one day. I have a studded dog collar round my neck and a poster of the Pistols in my room. I have been treated carefully since last year. They see me as an expensive vase, perhaps an ugly vase, but expensive all the same, and belonging to someone else. So they have to take special care of me. I am treated to things, things I wanted but was never allowed before. Things to keep me quiet.

I am six weeks pregnant; Venka gave birth two weeks ago. She asks no questions, is told only lies. I have been told many different stories since the last birth. Stories of experiments, DNA, cloning, genetics. These are words that float over my head. I really don't know what happens to them, the babies we make, the others we buy, but I have been told that their welfare is of paramount importance to 'the people' and that is something I choose to believe. So, now I have a client to see, I have a job to do. If you'll excuse me, I must go get changed, he wants the mother/baby thing.

Axis

She created something with a consciousness last night. She didn't mean to, but she was old enough and decent enough to accept responsibility for her mistakes. How was she to know that every mark on the graph plotted a similar pattern above her head, that the diametrics on her computer screen were at that moment rivalling a nine month gestation period in the sky?

Her mind had been elsewhere, heavy with real life, creating abstract images instead of the sales charts she was paid for. She missed Lee, ached for him. She had been counting the days till his return, counting down the number of times she woke up in the night and missed the rattle of his snoring, the way he always stole the covers, the way he never offered to make her a cup of coffee in the mornings. This was the first time they had been apart in four years of marriage and she found herself missing even the things that normally infuriated her, whilst the things that didn't usually bother her had become momentous in their gravity.

She had been drinking. Just a little red wine from an already-opened bottle. Enough to stain her thoughts a slightly damp carmine. Enough to push loneliness to the side a little. Draw the curtains, pour the wine and raise the stakes. Tapping at keys, figures, digits, an eternity of co-ordinates. The numbers becoming more like Chinese characters or Egyptian hieroglyphs as her ideas sloshed into being. Crosses and dots and curves becoming Cyrillic and maybe she had been looking to crack a code all along.

But it was so quiet. The inherited grandmother clock reminded her of her solitude, her heartbeat competing, almost as loud. Together they punctuated the silence and when she heard the sudden single cry of a baby she leapt out of her seat, sending the wine over the keyboard in a splash of dark red. Damn it, damn it. She switched off the machine and climbed into bed, which hadn't made it back into its other self as a sofa since Lee had gone. Fully clothed, a cigarette still smoking in the ashtray, the keyboard still dripping, the sound of that cry ringing in her ears like she had tinnitus. Cells dying, sound distorted.

It was still dark when she woke shivering. Usually she found the dark a comfort. Usually she had someone to share it with. But now it was just a hole too deep to climb out of. It was too early for bird song, too late for drunken revellers out on the street. It was just her and the universe, battling it out. She climbed out of bed and noticed the streaks of water on the skylight. Even the rain was silent, smudged against the glass. It was open, just a little, just a crack, enough to let in the cold. She reached up to pull it closed, arms bare white and goose-bumped, and that's when she saw it, up there, staring at her. She stared back for a moment, just stared. When it blinked her knees gave way and she fell to the floor.

She cried. She couldn't help it. The tears just came. The room was heavy with the vinegar smell of wine, the floor full of crumbs, strands of hair, dirty clothes. She could smell herself as she curled into a ball and hugged her knees. She could smell unwashed skin, old blood caked under fingernails, greasy hair plastered onto wet cheeks.

In the morning things were better. The light diffused everything. She was stiff, but she had made it through another night alone. Today Lee would be back and he would make everything right.

It was still looking at her, through the skylight. This time she didn't fall. She didn't even break her gaze for a long while. They looked at each other, its eyes dark brown and wet, the pupils huge. It looked sad. It was. . . she didn't know what it was. A planet? It looked like a planet, or a moon, a fat yellow disc taking up most of the sky and a corner of her skylight. It had no other features, no mouth, no body. It was a body in itself, a being, and she was sure she was the one who had created it. She sat down and let her mind stutter over the simple facts. She could find none. She could find nothing more than voodoo or sheer will or some kind of uterine stream of consciousness. Something miraculous. And now what? It seemed to be waiting for her to do something. But she was at a loss.

She decided to get dressed for the first time in two weeks. She went to pull her nightshirt over her head and released a foul reek of sweat, old and new. It buzzed around the room joining something more sour that may or may not have been emanating from inside her. She glanced up and saw those wretched eyes watching her every move and she became self-conscious, so she scooped up some clothes from the floor and bundled herself into the bathroom, easing the door closed, watching it looking at her.

The door latched quietly and she looked in the mirror. She wasn't too appalled. She looked the way she expected to, after not bathing or washing her hair for two weeks, a more transparent version of her former self. She was ex. She knew that. She was no longer what she had once been. She had gone through countless metamorphoses in her thirty three years. What difference could be made by one or two more? She cleaned her teeth and scrubbed at her yellowy tongue until it was raw. Spat blood into the grimy sink and then pulled on her clothes. They billowed like ship's sails, her hips were like a rack, her breasts hard white cushions, the areolae large and brailled and slightly sticky. She didn't bother with underwear. She didn't want to go into the bedroom to retrieve any. The door had remained closed for two weeks and some kind of instinct told her she didn't want to go in there now.

Dressed, as pointless an exercise as it seemed, she would at least be a little more kin to the wife Lee had said goodbye to fourteen days ago. The wife who had pleaded with him not to go, or to take her with him. The wife who was going stir-crazy being stuck at home, who missed her job, her colleagues, the cigarette breaks, the god-awful coffee from the machine in the staff-room. Dressed, she could greet him with a kiss. He could put a hand on the axis of her hip and ask her to walk towards him one more time. Sway for me, baby. Like you used to. Before. He would be tired, jet-lagged. She would loosen his tie, run him a bath, pour him a whisky. She would look after him, as was her desire. She would mother him a little, and then love him with her body. It was one of those things you never forgot how to do.

She sat on the chair by the computer, beneath the skylight. She tried to comb her hair but ended up yanking out whole clumps in a screech of agony and frustration. In the end she flung the comb across the room and waited. She would wait for him. He would see her.

"What do you want?" It didn't answer, because it couldn't. It could only stare.

"I don't know what to do," she told it. Or him.

"Stop looking at me."

But it wouldn't. She tried turning away, swivelled around in the chair so her back was to it, but she could still feel its burn and her eyes kept rolling up to meet those above her. Like she was drawn to it, helpless. She decided to accept that fate and sat until dark, when the planet changed its hue from the pale warmth of sour milk to a dandelion-yellow in the glow of the moon. And it blinked and it gazed and it did nothing more.

She didn't move until the sound of a key turning in the door made her jump. She was wet, her jeans piss-soaked. She didn't remember doing that. When she rose the odour of urine rose with her. Lee came through the door, his eyes heavy with grey shadows and his chin covered in rough dark stubble.

"You're up," he said. "It's late, it's after two. I thought you'd be asleep." He put down his bags and held out his arms. She didn't look at him. Just sat back down and looked back up. "It's okay," she whispered, tears beginning to trickle down her face.

"Liz?" He came over. Strode over in four easy steps. He kissed the top of her head, noticed the smell and his nose wrinkled in disgust before he could stop himself.

"Are you okay sweetheart? Where's Ryan?"

She pointed, a fleeting hand, a whispery bare finger reaching upwards towards the dark square of the skylight. "Look what I did," she said. "I didn't mean to. Isn't it amazing? At first I hated it, but now, I think, I'm quite proud. It has my eyes, don't you think?"

He looked up, squinted. "Liz, honey, I don't know what you're talking about. Where's Ryan? Is he asleep? Has he been good?"

She didn't answer him. She just ignored him, just kept staring up at empty sky. And what was that rotten smell? And then suddenly, he felt a stab in his heart. A pain, like he'd never felt before, the surge of something being ripped out, extinguished in an instant, lost, the worst possible death. He looked at his wife once more, before striding, running, over to the closed door. He threw it open and yelled "No! No no no no no!"

The violence of that time had been very real and not so long ago. Her body had retained the memory. The bloody mess on white sheets, the way her flesh had trembled and ripped and fought against the baby so goddamned hard when all she wanted to do was let the thing loose. Almost as violent as conception, when their two bodies had slammed together and will had ceased to dictate. She had opened up willingly like all those times before but she had still felt sacrificial, victim to his stabs and release. Of sounds let loose through clenched teeth and howling in the last respite and the way he moved her body this way and that as though, no really, she didn't want to be fucked like that. She did of course. This was only playing. All of it was only playing. It wasn't a reality until the tiny pink and white slippery emanation nine months later started to scream. . . more violently than anything she'd heard before. . . that she realised none of it had been a game after all. It's never obvious until you lose.

But now, there was silence.

And some awful chaotic stench coming from that room, that probed her gut and she dry-heaved a couple of times as it, that thing, watched sorrowfully from above and the clock chimed the half hour.

He was in there a long time. The wife knew what to expect so when he came stumbling out, snotty and teary and blank, holding that blue-black dislocated stinking bundle in his arms, she couldn't even act surprised. Simply, she turned to her computer, switched it on, and began to chart the new numbers that were crawling nimbly in her head.

The Suicide Room

Here, the land is untouched, the roads white with snow and the sun a bronze burn scar in the sky. Inside the Shogun Zeb and Catherine don't speak, each lost in their own thoughts, barely aware of the noise of the engine as it drowns out the tinny percussion from the radio.

They are close to the room now. Zeb knows it is near, although he cannot see it. With every bend in the road he expects it to be there in full view, but every corner reveals more snow, more blank nothingness. Could it be moving further away, daring them to keep driving through these bleak conditions, the silence that tries to envelop them?

God deserted this place a long time ago. The whole world is alone. Some say He died, others that He changed form in a magnificent evolutionary showdown. But the truth is not so fantastical. He just went away, faded, leaving us to suffocate in our own poisoned exhalations. He knew it would be genocide but He had a laugh anyway. Zeb has forgiven Him though and Zeb has a plan.

"You know you have to go in there alone, don't you?" He speaks without taking his eyes from the road.

Catherine nods. She is calm, not completely whole, but hardly fragmented. She looks at the firs, imagines a hundred diamante spider webs laced from branch to branch, beautiful, neglected. She does not know where they are going, she knows only what Zeb has told her, that this is a last attempt to save their marriage, their Gemini arrangement. So without question she is here. Should she meet her death today wrapped in the silk of these webs, she will be forever cocooned and left in the snow to melt to a former aquatic species and this is something she might have been waiting for.

At thirty she is always ready to put up a fight for her family. She has been a shelter for Zeb, and an outlet for his demands, tantrums and eventual melt-down. Through first sex and last sex she has sacrificed a lot for him. Her husband, her partner, her childhood sweetheart from her fourteenth year, the only one she loved, kissed, had sex with, has lost something. A part of him has become depleted, has been eaten away. Once, he was ravenous: for her, for work, for play, for life. But just in the last few months he has shut himself off from everything.

There are other rooms: on vertiginous mountain climbs like this, on the sand cushioned plains of Mongolia's Takla Makan Desert, by the hollowed out limestone gorges of Bosnia Herzegovina, through the chime and melody of a hot summer in Nepal, to the rush and density of a Canadian forest. But not one of these holds the same attraction for Zeb. He could pass any test, but to get to this room took all his strength. Now he is here to see if his wife can make the same journey, to see if she can stand it alone.

If Catherine gets through this she will join Zeb in the new world. No need for philosophy, no need for god, no need for science. And no need for physical touch. Having reached the highest echelons of spiritual existence they will have only to look down from their pivotal space, aware of their place in the macrocosm.

Zeb knows the room. He knows the feel of the door as it opens at his touch, he remembers the choking rush of familiarity that locked its hands around his throat and pulled him to esoteric depths. He knows Catherine will feel it too, and he knows she can do this; he has faith in her strength. He licks his lips which are chapped with the cold.

"Are you alright?" Catherine asks him. "You're very quiet."

He's quiet? These are the first words his wife has spoken since they got in the car. Zeb does not answer; he fiddles about with the radio to find a clearer signal but cannot even secure a prophecy.

"It could be suicide," Lee Wan had said, the day he took Zeb to the room.

35

"It's not a game, although it plays like one. You could be killing yourself, unaware that as you step over the threshold you're stepping over four thousand feet into nothing, putting a 38 calibre to your temple as you view the fixtures and fittings. Or it could be the most real thing you ever do."

Catherine does not know about Lee Wan; Zeb has not told her. She does not know about tragedy, instant death, instant truth; Zeb has not told her. To tell Catherine the risks would be to gamble with her faith in his instinct. And she needs to do this for Zeb's sake as well as for her own.

Zeb was a walking cadaver when he met Lee Wan in India nine months ago. Thirty five years old and none of his dreams realised. A wife he no longer cared for back in their hotel room, dyeing her hair to hide the premature grey, a son who hated him, who refused to leave his insect infested bed because he could not stand the heat, or the yellow food, or the hoards of local children who took his money and pulled hideous faces.

Dominic was finding out what it was like to be bullied and it did not rest easily on his nine year old shoulders. He had always carried a huge weight and unloaded it piece by piece onto the less fortunate kids at school. Zeb did not understand, back then, before the room. He did not remember being either bully or bullied as a child, and could not accept the demand for victimisation. Now Dominic was trying to bully his father into taking them back home but Zeb would not give in. He had gone to India an empty vessel, for help, to search for and befriend the Trimurti, to learn the secrets of dharma. And in a dusty street in New Delhi he had finally met Lee Wan.

With his caftan and bandana and blue-black beard Zeb thought Lee was a Turk. They had passed in the street but something had made them both double back to face one another. And they had begun to talk and had not stopped until the refinements of each man's life were known to the other as clearly as the level surface of a lake with its rotten detritus hidden below. Zeb learned that Lee was from Namp'o in North Korea, that he had spent twenty three years searching for moshka, the release from

36

reincarnation, and when his father died two years ago he had ended the search without conclusion and had stumbled upon the first room. One room had led to another had led to another. Lee Wan had visited them all.

Zeb wishes Lee Wan were here now. The fog has cleared considerably, the snow has ceased to fall and the calm of the sky seeps into the Shogun. In the distance he sees the room for the second time. He does not think Catherine has seen it yet. It rests on the mountainside as before. It has not moved. It remains windowless, nameless; its angles where wall meets wall are as painful as before, its stone work as smooth and cold as a sheet of metal. If Lee were here he would say something significant and reassuring, he could explain things to Catherine in a way to make her need this, to make her realise this is what she has been looking for. All Zeb can think of to say is,

"We're almost there."

The room holds no prisoners. Zeb would have offered himself wholly, would have sacrificed everything to stay. But as though it had plans of its own the room had ejected him back into the world. Zeb found the fear overwhelming but momentary, and then the whole world blossomed.

Lee Wan had tried to persuade Zeb to visit the other rooms first, but could see he was wasting his time. Zeb was determined to go straight to the top. So, six months ago, he had taken Zeb to Romania, to the Carpathians where at 4018 feet above sea level stood the Suicide Room, so called because of its statistics.

The room is whatever you don't know you want it to be. It is neither gilded nor filled with precious stones; it is not an orgy of flesh or the place to make three wishes. It is not based on desire or a latent wish-fulfilment. Its power is taken from what is not seen, from the deepest whorls of the occupant's psyche. Were that person to leave the room and find an audience of 70 thousand rising to their feet in a standing ovation, he would not be surprised. Should he pass himself walking up the mountain as he makes his descent, this would fill him only with the urge for a 'good day' and a wry smile. For the room shares all your secrets and will not push you out until it has shown you everything you need to know.

It was a day much like this when Zeb opened the door to the room and Lee Wan turned and began his descent of the mountain. Freezing cold, snow storms, frost bitten toes and cold white breath. He did not have a vehicle then. He and Lee had hitched a ride half way and walked the rest. And as he turned the handle on the door Lee had walked away and Zeb had never seen him again.

The first thing he saw was the open fire. Drawn to the heat and the colour after the white and grey of the outdoors he knelt beside it to thaw out. He had not noticed a chimney and did not question who had stoked the flames. He was just glad to find warmth in a room that looked to hold no secrets. He sat close to the fire and let the purring of gold flames lull his heavily beating heart, before looking around to take in his surroundings.

On the far wall hung a picture at a slant that beckoned to be straightened. Zeb recognised the yellow dog as Sandy, the golden retriever he'd had as a boy. He would have been about Dominic's age when he was given the pup. He had been misbehaving; not bullying like Dom, but turning the wheel onto himself, in the guise of curiosity. His parents had bought him the dog to placate him, to give him a taste of responsibility, to bring him out from the depths of his silence, his misery. The doctor had labelled him autistic but he wasn't. He was just more comfortable in his own reality. A year later the dog was dead. Zeb put rat poison in its food and watched with interest when Sandy began to buck and urinate and foam dripped from his open mouth. He was never given another pet. He had forgotten about Sandy until now.

There was another picture. His mother, his younger brother Charlie and himself on a beach in Nice. His father was not included in the shot as he was on the other side of the camera. Standing captive now before this snatched moment of tranquillity, a small black mass like ink

38

began to coat his tongue. It grew, snow-balled tumbleweed rabid into a poison that he could not swallow. He licked his lips. There were memories here, attached to this picture, that he could not quite recall. Bad memories. And the mass was growing.

He coughed and swallowed and the tumour slid down his throat like an oyster, like mucus into his gut and the sting on his legs and the pain in his head was remembered in a hundred lashes. The poison in his stomach reared like horses and he was in the sea, in the currents of the Mediterranean, holding Charlie under the blue to see how long the boy can hold his breath, to see him thrash his arms and legs, to see if he changes colour. He is about to let go when the boy stops moving and then his mother and father are on him, his mother screaming and his father pulling him away, hurting, almost yanking his arm out of the socket. Then somebody is giving Charlie mouth to mouth and the young boy coughs up a lungful of water and sits up and cries and Zeb gets the worst beating of his life.

And with this memory came a hundred more, and a thousand regrets. And the room changed from the Winnie the Pooh sanctuary of a three year old boy, through the richness of blue and green and an aeroplane mobile to circle overhead, through the hard white sympathy of a hospital bed, to dark painted walls of an adolescent hell, to adulthood, to now, to over and over in dizzying kaleidoscopic colours and zero gravity so Zeb was floating with ghosts, his mother, his father and brother shaking their heads and pointing their fingers; the brown eyes, the heavy lids, the choking, the wailing all reached him even when he covered his ears and sat on the floor with his eyes squeezed shut, fifteen years old and waiting for the bite of his father's belt.

When he heard the rhythm of a woman's heavy breathing he looked up. He was sitting at the foot of a hospital bed and he could see Catherine, tears on her flushed cheeks, sweat on her forehead, heavily pregnant. Doctors in green closed in around her and he could not see. They were telling her to push. He could not see; they would not let him near. He had missed the birth of Dominic, had been . . . elsewhere. But later he had regretted this, had hated seeing Catherine's face that said, 'How could you be so unkind, to miss the birth of the only child I will ever give you, to be away when I need you most' even though her voice said, "It's okay, you're here now."

She was screaming his name. He could see her long fingers wrenching the air, trying to grab him even though he was miles away. Even though he wasn't. He was here now and she did not realise because she could not see him. He would not miss it a second time.

He heard a baby cry. The group of doctors parted. The one wearing the red-stained gown placed a bundle in Zeb's hands. The purple face and swaddled body was Dominic. Zeb looked at Catherine. She smiled and for the first time he knew what it was to be needed.

They have arrived. It has been hours. It has been a lifetime. Catherine looks at Zeb searchingly as he kills the engine but he does not look at her. There are tears threaded in her lashes and he knows she is trying desperately not to cry. But this is no time for emotion. He has parked close enough to watch her walk over to the room, but far enough to not see the expression on her face when she comes out. He is afraid for her but they have arrived and to turn around now would be a small death. And Catherine will have too many questions. So he urges her on, tells her everything is fine, that she has nothing to fear. And as she turns the handle and steps into the room without looking back he only hopes there are no dark secrets hidden beneath the surface that she had never dared to share.

And then he sits and waits, and waits and waits.

The Seedy Underbelly

Deep inside the stomach . . . No, further down, below, to the very pit where the flesh swells a little in a rounded mass and the skin is softer, less taut. Here, where it can be grabbed between thumb and finger to roll it or stretch it. It stretches like this for a reason of course. A fleshy baby-making reason. But she isn't born for this so she doesn't need the apparatus.

Might as well chisel them out sideways.

Mostly there is just a churning down there, down near the fine whiskers. It's where her anger begins with a pulse before it rises to the throat. It's where the giddiness is born at the sight of *him*, and later *him* and every other *him*. Pretty flicking rickety spinning spiders making dirty webs sore with the craving. It is pure emotion. The stomach tells of hunger, the throat of thirst, the skin of heat, the heart of. . . nothing. Except fear perhaps. Love lies in the pit, along with hate and sadness and sometimes joy. All the debris floating around in the darkest dark. But mostly it just churns.

She is thirsty but water does not solve it. Milk turns to cream and whisky lets loose the loneliness. It's a darker juice she craves. Something thick like treacle that might coagulate like blood. So she steps into the shed where the mice snigger, and grabbing the can of motor oil, she tips it to her lips and drinks. Hoping it will stop the gritty churning. She sits on the wooden floor and waits for quiet, in the brown dirt and the sharp silver prongs of the gardening tools that lean heavily against the back wall. Her hands sweep over wood and splinters, and splinters and splinters itching, which squeeze themselves into the soft pads of her fingers like burrowing insects.

She doesn't have long to wait before the things inside of her begin to change their path, the churning reduced to a brick-upon-brick smoothness or the teeth of cogs catching in the teeth of other cogs. She feels the buzz and hum of the machine. The bulk of it presses against her lower back, leaving a dent, and she doesn't know whether to hunch over or sit on the floor with legs bent and scabby knees pointing to opposite walls. Sick, weighty, it pulls and tugs at her until suddenly her body lurches forwards and she plunges into a kind of black oblivion and the contents of her stomach pool from her stretched lips and onto the floor in a sticky brown splash of bile and the clank of nuts and bolts, springs, screws, nails, blades that scratch at her throat.

Sore, spent, relieved, she gathers up the pieces (stringy with saliva) in her hands and begins to jigsaw them together into a gritty neonate. An adorable little thing with a knife blade grin, a handle in its back and bulbs for eyes that light up when it's hungry.

Solid Gold

I adore beautiful things. Defining myself by their glossy parameters is as natural to me as believing in their illusion, believing in the fairy tale reflection of my made-up face. It was in my late teens and early twenties when I began harbouring desires to adorn myself and my immediate surroundings with elegance and style. I started to watch my posture and my language, remembering to say 'I don't know' rather than 'dunno'. But when it came to my surroundings, elegance proved more difficult to accomplish.

Rented accommodation at a price I could afford meant stuffy little bed-sits above shoe shops and sweet-smelling bakeries, where every night I dreamt of flames thrashing at my door. But I did what I could to make these places more attractive. A wardrobe pushed into the corner to cover the damp patches of mould, black and white prints of Veronica Lake and Rita Heyworth on the walls, a bunch of carmine roses on the chest of drawers, and a purple drape over the cabinet to hide the pinprick holes left by woodworm. I used to sew lace onto my clothes, fancy buttons and pieces of silk, and spray them with perfume to counteract the musty smell that would linger anyway.

But now it is easier. Now that I am thirty-five and I own a perfect little flat with its wooden floors, ostrich feathers adorning the walls, blinds at the windows instead of curtains that don't shut properly and a glass shower door instead of a blackening plastic curtain that I ripped down when I fell in the bath, drunk.

I went out a lot when I was younger. I drank, I smoked, I took men home to bed. I don't drink or smoke anymore. I can't stand the smell of it on my clothes and in my hair. And if I bring a man home now I make him leave his shoes at the door and I change the bed sheets that very same night. I cannot stand to wake up next to a man to remind me of my lack of self-respect. Yes, I still take strangers home but at least I can forget about them the next morning and begin the day like some newly born virgin. Alone.

Still, I've been wondering lately, as my waist has begun to thicken and the fine lines around my eyes and mouth have become less fine, thinking, wondering, pondering in moments of loneliness whether any of this is worth it.

Sometimes I want to sweep my hands across the coffee table, sweep it clear of the neatly stacked magazines, knock the green glass vase to the floor so it smashes in a bloom of acrid-smelling water; crush the daffodils beneath my feet, take pleasure in destroying something so beautiful. Vibrant yellow scented and soft, yet dead by all accounts. Stupid flowers trying so hard to keep on living even after they've been ripped from the soil.

Sometimes I imagine taking the crystal glasses from the kitchen and smashing them, risking tiny splinters shooting into my face like gold-dust.

Sometimes the intensity of my yearning to destroy surprises me.

I could eat a slab of chocolate cake and let the crumbs fall silently onto the floor to get trodden into the bedroom carpet in doughy lumps like chewing gum, and then wipe my sticky hands on my nightdress. I might blow my nose and throw the damp snot-filled tissue onto the floor instead of tossing it into the bin.

Not that I would ever do any of these things. As much as I hate to admit it, I need these objects and this routine. I can't afford to let slip my restraint. After the adrenaline rush, it would mean the loss of everything. The anti-climax would prove too much to bear. These are my constants, my stability, when I myself am mutable. It is this very reasoning that has kept me from 'settling down'. Despite my age I can still attract the attention of men in the street; a man will still begin to sing as he sidles past me; the young shop assistant in the newsagents where I buy my daily newspaper still attempts to flirt with me as he hands over my grubby change. But these men just seem so. . . what is it? They seem so soft, physically and mentally. All rippling muscle or well-formed fat, idly supportive or downright idolatrous, there is nothing there for me. I need solidity. I need a pillar or a great bed of soil to keep me rooted.

I love all of this flat, but my bedroom is my favourite place, my sanctuary. Its white carpet is like sand, ruffling my bare feet, or my freshly-shaven legs when I choose to lie there, for sometimes it offers more comfort than the tightly-made bed. I sleep well but when I wake, the sheets are often still stretched tightly across and the pale gold coverlet still flat, never rumpled, never hanging off the end or bunched up on the floor. The walls are painted a pale carnation colour, the wardrobe is a deep velvet mahogany. Wooden slats at the window keep the world outside or with a whim admit the sun. And my favourite spot to sit, the large bay windowsill, is adorned with silk, velvet, and fur cushions in matching creams and ochre.

I like to sit there and read, sometimes delighting in the flow of words. Other times I pick out phrases and re-write them in a more pleasing way. I did start writing a novel once, but found it impossible to continue with my ever-fluctuating rush of ideas, which would change course so often I might have ended up writing ten novels within the confines of a single book jacket.

It was fun for a time, though. At work I would note down snippets of conversation, interesting phrases, whispered affections between doctor and nurse, diluted truths between doctor and patient. People can say the most interesting things in fleeting moments, when they think nobody is listening. I used to bring the notes home and stick them around the flat. The stolen lines scribbled onto post-its, headed with the names of various medicines that sounded like exotic blooms; Acyclovir (for STDs), Meridia (obesity), Starlix (diabetes). But one day I tore down those post-its and threw the novel into remission. I was wasting my time, thinking the discipline of novel-writing could pin me down when in fact it had begun to devour me.

I sit here now, on the windowsill, reading Simone de Beauvoir and looking out at the park while the scent of sandalwood sends its lazy tendrils to permeate my hair and clothes and the pores of my skin. It is quiet today. Joe must be out for there is no thrumming or vibrating shaking my floorboards from his stereo downstairs. I prefer the stillness you can only get from a quiet room. Music creates a sense of movement, as though I can actually feel the notes pervading the air.

It's not a particularly attractive park that I look down on. From my fourth floor window I can see the empty crisp packets and coke cans spilling out of the bins, and I often see dogs squatting while their owners smoke cigarettes before walking away, leaving a solitary lump of excrement in their wake.

The path directly below my window has become a dumping ground. I don't know who first decided to leave a bulging heap of black binbags there but now people have decided to follow suit, leaving an old TV with a smashed screen, a battered blue cot, a black umbrella hunched up and wing-jutted like an injured bird, and something else which must have been left last night. It has caught my eye because the sun is glinting off its metal surface, but I'm not actually sure what it is. It just looks like a hunk of metal, but it hums with a strange message. I feel almost enamoured by its come-hither cool, its hard-to-get transparency. In an unfathomable moment of decisiveness I jump from the windowsill and run to the door.

It's cold. It's Sunday morning and the park is empty but for a couple of joggers who pay me no heed as they run past, breathing heavily into their bitty conversation. I linger in front of the object. I see now that it is not simply a cube of smooth metal but made up of several components. It is in fact an engine. Somewhere, a car has been crudely gutted. One side, the side I couldn't see from the window, is red and orange and smeared with black oil over rusty hinged segments. There are fat and thin tubes like ligaments connecting all over the machine, like the arteries tracing the pig heart I remember from school. I am fascinated with this metal body of work, its craftsmanship. Without thinking, I place the palms of my hands

46

flat against the metal, almost expecting to feel a slight vibration, an oozing of warmth. But it is cold and still like a corpse. I wonder if the heat of my hands might seep through, or would its chill prove stronger?

"Ahem."

I turn to see Joe paused at the front door, key in hand, staring at me. I guess I must look strange in my cotton nightdress, but I haven't noticed the cold and it is only now that I see the fuzz of blonde hairs standing up on my arms.

I smile. "Well, don't just stand there," I say. "Give me a hand."

I don't know how we manage it but we get the engine into the lift and across to my front door.

"Shoes off, please," I say, sliding out of my own.

We drag it inch by inch, puffing and blowing shallow breaths with sweat beading our skin, across the floor and into the bedroom. We stop and Joe raises his eyebrows as he leans against the door frame. I look at my nightdress. It is filthy with black grease and a thread has pulled free, leaving a line of fabric tugging at the hem. I pull it back into place with my dirty hands and motion to the front door.

He might be after a kiss, sex, a cup of tea and a cake, or all of the above, but I don't want him messing up my flat any longer. If he had thrown himself onto me I probably would not have rejected him, he is a good looking young man after all, but he reminds me of myself in so many ways. The way I was at his age, the way I am now. It's obvious he came from the same dirty, common working-class roots as myself. It's not snobbishness on my part, of this I am adamant. It is an unwillingness to go back to what I have spent the last fifteen years struggling out of, like a tight-fitting skin. It is only occasionally that I wonder what a person does once all their dreams are fulfilled.

"Thanks. Goodbye," I say. Joe puts on his shoes to leave and soon I hear him downstairs with his rock music and his skulking.

I don't know why I wanted this damn thing. I look at it, so out of place, taking up half the space in my room. There is a thick track mark leading from the machine to the front door. The white carpet flattened and inky black, and the metal door tread has come loose where part of the carpet has been dragged out and left a gap big enough for a mouse to crawl under. My hands feel gritty and there are flakes of rust between my fingers. I feel disgusting. But somehow I don't care. I won't wash my hands and I won't take off this nightdress yet. And when I do, I won't throw it away but hang it back up in the wardrobe instead.

I pick up my book and lie on the bed, trying to read, trying to ignore the music from downstairs. But my gaze keeps wandering. Keeps moving slyly from the page to the engine sitting there on the floor like a piece of modern art.

So I roll off the bed and scuff my way into the kitchen, remembering I haven't eaten yet and it is getting on for one o'clock. I have no food in the cupboards, and don't remember when I last went shopping. I barely eat at home anymore, but in the freezer I discover half a loaf and after prizing apart a couple of slices I stick them in the toaster.

I carry the hot buttered toast in my hands, back into the bedroom. I sit on the bed and devour them, staring at the engine. The crumbs fall onto my lap and I shake them onto the floor absent-mindedly; tiny buds of yellow and brown that mingle with the colours carefully chosen a few years before.

The rest of the day is spent in some kind of disarray. Is it a lethargy I feel, an ennui? Is it the onset of a belated winter depression? I seem unable to concentrate on any one thing, and the music from downstairs is beginning to grate on my nerves. It's getting into my blood and running rough-shod through every artery, thumping with a voodoo precision.

With nothing better to do I climb into bed and feel sleep pulling at me like a tide, pushing me back and forth between oceanic depths and shallow pools, waking me momentarily before pulling me under once more. I am a drowning woman. It is while beneath the surface, passing through downstreams and warm currents, that I begin to hear a different kind of music. Subdued at first, and distorted like a gramophone record far into the distance. But it is getting clearer, and louder, as though I were moving closer to it.

Except I am not moving. I am simply being, with limbs floating as if held by string. Out of the dark it comes in a dull halo of light. Like a creature of the sea, some blind, silver-bellied monster of fictional proportions. And there am I, right behind it, behind the engine which has become an organ and I am the starlet grinding out the music. Turning the handle to make the seismograph roll, the keys jumping over the lumps and bumps in the shape of musical notes. And there, sitting on my shoulder is a small capuchin monkey, dressed in a blue waistcoat, nibbling on my ear and wearing Joe's superfluous grin.

I wake with a shudder. The engine still sits where I left it. I see the outline of its solid form in the now-darkness. I blink. It stares. I grab the gold coverlet from the bed and spread it neatly on the floor, pull it flat, ensure the corners are not folded, smooth out the crumples. Then, with all my strength, I strain and push and heave the engine onto it. It folds one corner and crumples the smoothness.

I push him onto his side with a crash, and then I lie down next to him. From below, Joe's heavy music begins. Like me, he cannot sleep. Usually I would be roiling with anger at this intervention but tonight it seems right. It provides a canvas for this scene, thunderous and ominous and consciously non-human.

I feel him hum as I touch him, thrumming my name. I wonder if he is thinking of me now. I stretch one arm uncomfortably around his silver body, close my eyes like a spent lover, and let myself drift into restful sleep.

Fly

It was all in the wrist action. No need to wave one's arms about like a mad man. It was a quick, sharp flick of the carpus. A sudden convulsion after a calculated appraisal of the target's next move.

Raynard shuffled onto his back and waved the swat to and fro in front of his face, enjoying the swoosh of air as it rushed through the perforations. These flies were driving him insane. And the heat, and the stench of lodged flesh on the bed, like week-old food stuck between two back teeth. Neither of them had moved off the bed in days, except to piss and get another tub of ice cream from the freezer. The last had turned to a warm pink sludge and a couple of flies floated in there, ending their sticky fight in creamy strawberry and vanilla. They didn't come in through the open window though, as one might expect. They came in through the plug sockets.

Raynard had watched them in horror as they poured in through the holes in the wall. Just the one empty socket. If the others hadn't been in use, they would probably be pouring their black mass through those too. They crawled on Lydia's back and she didn't even bother to swipe them anymore. She just lay there, snoring, drooling, a beached beast, occasionally hefting herself over an inch causing the flies to jump off as one, before landing back down on the sweating white flesh.

There was one now, on her buttocks. Green shiny body, a slow, lazy mover this one, sliding over the large grey sheet of her knickers. Raynard could get that one. He had it in his sights. It was a careful operation, no need to rush. You had to know your enemy, put yourself in the mind of the fly. It was like a game of chess. You had to figure out its moves. He kept his eye on it, watched it twitch with a low buzz like an electric razor switching on and off. He raised the swat. Slowly. . . slowly.

Raised it above his head. Watch it. . . slowly. And THWACK. He brought it down right on the left cheek.

"Argh!" she bellowed. "You fuck!"

Lydia's plump buttock glowed a red square, but there was no fly corpse. The damn thing had outwitted him, had flown at the last moment.

"Shit!" Raynard jumped off the bed.

Lydia had fallen quiet again, had barely moved. The gurgle of saliva passing up her throat vomiting out something that might have been words. It was all she was capable of.

Once she might have jumped out of bed and wrestled him, wrestled the fly swat out of his hands and with giggles attempted to attack him, to roll off the bed with feet tangled in the sheet and a tickle and a kiss and maybe he would slip his hand between her legs and find a wetness there. And he could kiss her large open mouth and their teeth would bang together and lying on top of an empty food carton he would heave himself inside her and make some kind of love to her.

But the bottle of valium by the side of the bed was almost empty and she was snuggling her nose back into the dirty pillow to embrace sleep once again. Swollen lids almost covering the double-winged beasts reflected over and over in milky blue pupils.

He still had his sights on the fly. It thought he couldn't see it, nestled in the folds of the curtain. Deftly he crept on the dirty balls of his naked feet. Quietly he inched. The fly waited now. It was on the curtain rail. One foot on the sill, a ninja, his shorts clinging to the fair hair on his thighs, his chest exposed, scratched with holes, insect bites. Bed bugs, mosquitoes, fleas, tics, mites, they were all the same. Feeding off him. Feeding off Lydia. Repulsive. He reached up. A back hand? An over arm. Front crawl. He was swimming through air. Reached back and up. And as he did so his foot slipped. He thought, as he crashed through the open window and flapped his arms, how ironic. As his dark shape went tumbling through the void in slow motion and his fingers grabbed onto the window's edge. If Lydia would just turn, just wake and turn and see him for one last second before he fell.

"Lydia."

He let go. Atrophied muscles, his arms too weak to carry his weight, his palms too slick to stick.

He might count the stories. One two three. . . fifteen sixteen. But was too busy thinking about his fate. It was a slow fall. Slow and lazy. She would wonder where he was, if she woke for just a moment. She would feel a cool hollow at her back, a dent where he had lain. If she woke. If the bugs didn't simply devour her.

He landed with a crash onto the vendor. The man who sold plastic name tags, all for one person. Zola. Each one the same four letter word. Who was Zola anyway?

It was his last thought before he ended his sticky flight in blood oozing over the pavement like raspberry sauce.

The Bride Stripped Bare

A horse lies broken in her dream street, slack-bellied, white-eyed, not-yet dead, but near enough. Figures come running from shadows and street corners, and from the darkness beneath. Some carry knives. Others come baring tooth and claw. Starvation has brought out the beast in everyone. They tear into the horse's belly and it rasps a death rattle as blood oozes between their dirty fingers. Some stick their heads straight into the wound to grab at intestines with their stinking teeth, letting the blood mat their beards, a sticky scarlet sauce. They're so hungry, when the best muscles and organs have gone, they don't stop. The bladder is torn apart, the nose ripped off, eyeballs fought over.

The woman stirs in her sleep. Her body twists. On her back she moans a little. Adam watches her, wide awake. He hasn't slept all night.

In the dream she becomes the horse. Or the horse becomes her. It takes on her form and she is lying on wet cobbles while the beasts feed on her. And they, too, are changing. Mutating. From dirty-skinned humans to birds feathered in black, gold beaks flecked with red. Like vultures they pull at her insides, tug at the meat there like pulling a worm from soil. Claws open up her belly, her womb, her junctions. Piercing thin membrane, the fluid lies still, refuses to run. The foetus inside opens its eyes and glares.

In the dream her fingers tighten around the soft smooth coldness of the egg now sitting in her palm. It is light brown and rounded like her own belly. With a sudden urge, a thrust like a nervous tic, her fingers clench, the digits closing around the orb like there is no choice, like it might just squeeze itself between the webbing, as though it might shoot out of her hands like an oily newborn. But, of course, it breaks. And her hands are washed with blood.

She sits up. Her body is wet with sweat, wanting to slide away from the hot skin of the host beside her. No, she is the host now. She kicks back the cover, nightdress clinging to her damp patches. Her belly tight and stretched to its capacity, full to the gullet, the throat, rapidly wanting to drizzle up and out of the corners of her mouth. He snores. She feels alone even though she has been in close company for the past eight months.

It is a huge effort to climb out of bed. Her swollen stomach clamps her movements, holds her down for a moment until she gains balance and uses her palms flat on the bed to push her weight forward. Adam doesn't know if she's aware of him awake beside her, so he just watches, quietly. She fascinates him. His wife of three years, their first child inside her. He has watched her grow, swell with flesh and blood. The consummation. The offering. The time might be perfect. They just need to wait for stillness, she says.

"Will it ever stop?" Her palms pressed against the cool glass of the window pane are wet, her fingertips dance across her reflection where the moon is a sliver between her eyes. She is unmoving and part of the scenery, part of the outside, that void, a pretty trompe l'oeil. He pulls back the duvet with its warm imprint of her heavy body.

"Come back to bed," he murmurs. He doesn't want her distressed. Her frame of mind is as important tonight as anything beyond the hotel room. The weather, the planets, the river, especially the river. This is their third and last night in the hotel. For three days they have been watching the river. Standing at the window, sitting on its banks, dipping fingers in the cold rush. At breakfast she doesn't eat, but she can surely feel the stares of the three other guests. She is pregnant after all. She's a diamond. She holds a secret no one else here holds. But she isn't happy. She isn't excited. She is sad. She is quiet. She wants for nothing but the river to stop. It's all she ever asks. When? When will it stop? And he can't answer because he doesn't share her faith.

He doesn't see the streaks on the window from her bloody fingers.

Any river will do. It doesn't have to be the Tavy. But this is the place Anne wanted to come to. Five months into the pregnancy she started talking of the river. Only when the river ceases to flow will they come. These creatures of myth and horror story. The creatures Adam had never heard of and would never have believed in. But her desire to come here, the tears, the tantrums when he said no. She pulled out her hair till her scalp bled, she pulled out her lashes till her eye lids swelled to twice their size. She screamed and kicked and bit him until he said, Fine. Okay, I can't cope with this. I will be here for you. I will take you to the river. I will even comfort you when the river continues to flow. Just don't ask me to believe in your nonsense. And then she had fallen silent, and she had asked for nothing more.

She lies in his arms now, stiff and cold. She doesn't wriggle from his grasp like a cat or push at his body with her nails. She just lies there and allows him to hold her. Eventually her body begins to relax, to soften. Her eyelids linger for a moment over the whites, before closing completely, tightly, to hold in the visions. And the temperature in the room begins to drop.

It's the twenty-third of June. The baby (Michael? Adam? Jennifer?) is due on the twentieth of July. The middle of summer. They have been walking about in shorts and t-shirts. Anne's expanding belly has been showing beneath the hem of her shirts as they have shrunk back, upwards towards her breasts. Her thighs are not as firm as they were since she stopped working out, but they are beautiful all the same. Adam has spent the early summer sweating over those thighs, wanting to lick them, kiss them, just to lay a finger on them, but she hasn't let him and until the screaming tantrums began, he put it down to hormones. Now he believes there is something seriously wrong with his wife. He fears he will be bringing up a baby alone, and caring for a woman too disturbed to even look after herself.

As the temperature drops, he presses himself closer to her. Aware, even in his sleep, of her non-responsiveness, but glad of the chance for proximity. And she, feeling the cold, perhaps lets herself be drawn to his heat, that perfect 37.5 degrees she used to feel in the droplets of sperm between her thighs, in his blood when she bit his mouth kissing too passionately, in the tears he shed when she first fought his refusal.

The wallpaper in the room is white with pink roses. The bedspread is caramel. There is an off-white teasmaid next to his side of the bed, a brown television set with an indoor aerial and a bulbous screen. The room, the whole hotel, is set apart in time. Stuck in allegory or history. Or some other story. It doesn't seem to belong anywhere.

Shadows that start off as wispy grey deepen to charcoal as they flit around the room. Sliding between cracks, oozing from behind the wallpaper, especially in the bottom corner where it is coming away from the wall. They dance in the corners, shrink back from the open window with its river-wet breeze that flutters the lace hanging over the edges of the bedside table. Between the wooden slats of the bed and the coils in the mattress. They penetrate the walls like greasy stains, and everything becomes blotted out with their foetid black stink.

Beyond the window, tree branches knock against the stone wall of the house, tapping like devils claws to enter. They burn to black and smash against windows as though a fierce wind has suddenly whipped up from nowhere and is bending the boughs like balloons into sinister animal shapes, the hedges below learning topiary, transforming themselves into monsters, and above, like a swarm of bees, birds circle and scream.

3am hits and a collective sigh is whispered from each and every guest. Each breath is a puff of smoke from lips chapped beneath noses red and dripping. Soon there will be no life at all. Teeth chatter. Hairs stand up on flesh, a meagre defence against the cold. A mottled and dirty cat outside breathes its last. Flowers are closed up, never to re-open. Wild rabbits curl up and die, even in the warmth of their burrows. And the birds continue to circle.

Over the next hour, the river begins to slow. Lumps of ice like miniature bergs form and swill in the heavy current. Finally, the river freezes. Sighs and breathes its last. In the field on the other bank a horse collapses and dies, legs kicked straight into the air, its nostrils wide and cooling, tail lifted and stomach bulging. Massively pregnant, its genitalia is swollen and red, protruding, trying to expel something that will never let go. Two bodies frozen, one inside the other.

Anne opens her eyes. There is a pounding in her head and behind the walls of her womb, a ramming, a banging, a forcing its way out. The first cracks split the solid surface of the river. A sudden thawing, spring, lambing season, within seconds. The drip drip drip of water wanting to flow, and beneath Anne's thighs, a body of water is soaking the mattress.

"Adam" she yells, and pushes his chest with her fist. He wakes immediately, alarmed.

"My water's broken. Shit. Adam."

He jumps out of bed, wincing at stiffened joints, lunging through the door and into a silent corridor. Towels, hot water, something to put it in. Another person. That's what he needs. Someone else to share this with because, shit! his wife is having a baby and he doesn't know what to do. But all he finds are locked doors and an empty reception. There is not a person to be seen. Just the loud gunfire chattering, laughing almost, of a charm of magpies poking around the desk. Eight of them, jutting and preening and staring, though the front door is firmly shut and the windows closed for the night.

He returns empty-handed. Anne is a silhouette on the bed, scrunched up around the mound of her belly which seems almost like a separate part of her. There's Anne. And then there's this fleshy extension that causes backache and tears and swollen breasts and rages.

"I'll call someone," he says. "A hospital." But even as he is picking up the receiver to a dead line she's screeching "No!" in a desperate, high-pitched wail.

He has anticipated this. She has said all along that there would be no need for midwives, hospitals, gowns, forceps, any of that. She would give birth at home in her most comfortable, familiar surroundings, where she would be able to bond instantly with their baby. But this is too fast. This is too early. Unexpected. And there is blood on the palms of her hands. Her legs are spread wide and her bloody nails are scratching downwards across her belly, as though this manic rhythm might cause her to expel.

This is the moment. Adam takes one of her hands in his and presses the fingers tenderly, but she recoils and puts her hand back into place on her stomach. This is what she has been waiting for. This is the moment when she will give birth to their son or daughter and Adam must either witness her disappointment, which will be as heart-rending for him as for it will be for her. Or he must play along with her hope of a bright future. Because according to her myth, her story, their baby will have been blessed by those who come only when running water stills. But this might not be obvious from the start, she had told him. Their child will be gifted, but these things won't show until the child is old enough to communicate, to learn and create.

She is breathing rapidly, almost chanting with the rhythm, her whole body pulsating. He is simply waiting, redundant. Looking out of the window at the horse on its back, dead and pregnant. He has to turn away, and when he looks back at the bed he sees the blood beneath her thighs and the look on Anne's face. It's a look of horror, of a dawning realization that things are not as they should be. The river flows, the blood forges its own path, and Anne pushes and pushes with all her might, wanting now to get the thing out of her and hoping, just hoping, that this is all part of the natural course.

The river is beginning to sound like rapids, white water foaming like a rabid animal. The birds still circle. Occasionally they dive and soar to break the momentum, but stray birds always rejoin the flock. And from beneath the bed, a rook creeps out, black eyes darting, white beak tipped in black, feathers sleek. It hops forward, into the light, onto the windowsill, and it watches the chaos on the bed.

It will take just one more shove, an almighty heave, to finally push the baby out. Anne is preparing for it, for a bone-splitting shudder, for the feeling of insides being torn out. For that moment of relief.

And there it is. The baby puddles out onto the wet bed under cover of blood and mucus. Three, maybe four seconds pass before Adam comes to his senses and rushes over, looks at Anne, and picks up the tiny bundle. It really is small, very small, and sticky with grime. He swaddles the thing (boy? girl?) in a hotel towel, turning it red, and tries to delicately wipe the eyes and mouth, clear the airways, hear a cry. Only then does he begin to see the shape of things. The mouth's protrusion, the random feathers piercing the body like needles jutting from veins, the webbed fingers and four toes, one extending backwards to the heel of each foot. This is a travesty. The eyes are black. One on each side of the head. And the beak is fleshy and pink. It doesn't breathe.

He looks at Anne. She looks at the window. Through it she is watching the birds as they disappear, the whole flock an upwards pointing V, shooting through the clouds like a rocket. She turns to Adam and lets out an horrendous scream and the rook in the room circles once before flying headlong into the windowpane and falling dead to the floor.

You're. . .

. . . poetry in motion. You're part of an ensemble that makes up three quarters space and one quarter iron fist. If I could only see your hands. But as part of this *mise en scène* only a third of you is in my line of vision. On your knees you are framed by the bathroom door which stands wide open, framed by the bedroom, and then by the window through which I watch you: the final frame. And the first.

I only came out here to smoke a cigarette. I could smoke in my motel room. It's air-conditioned in there. I could lie on the bed and stare at the wall where the remnants of a squashed something have left a dark brown stain. I could contemplate. But I've contemplated too much already. Besides, I hate smoking indoors. I don't really want this cigarette but it has become part of my ritual. One cigarette in every new motel. And a hole burnt through the map with the red hot tip. There are five holes in it now and it has a comforting smell to it. Five motels, five different towns, but none have piqued my curiosity like this one. Like you.

I guess you're kneeling at the bath. Or perhaps I should say tub. While on this cross-country tour of America I may as well pick up some of the lingo. You're kneeling on the white tiled floor, facing the tub, and your arms are moving in a rhythm. I can only think you're washing something: scrubbing. Your shirt sleeves are rolled up and I see the muscles in your arms dance like bugs beneath the skin. I could watch this movement all night. But then you turn. Something has caught your attention. It is too late to duck. You have seen me. I watch you stand and walk towards me.

The map is a crushed up and disintegrating wad in my back pocket. It lives close to my body always. I really *would* be lost without it. Why does an opened map never fold back up properly? It's like a door that can never be closed, a path that can never be travelled more than once. Or something less poetic. When people pick up that I'm 'not from around here' they ask where I am going and where I have been. Visiting friends? Working? Sight-seeing? I say yes to whatever they suggest. I am everything and everyone to these strangers. I am whatever they want me to be.

To be honest, I don't really know what I'm doing. I never asked. I just saved, scraped, and stole enough money for escape and took the first opportunity that came along. If anyone were to ask what I was escaping from, I wouldn't be able to put it into words. It would sound too much like a cliché. I am not missed. I know that much. I am not sought. And nobody will have thought to check the obituaries.

When you open the door you question me with your stare, but say nothing. You are frowning but not in anger. The fleeting fear that this might be the last burn hole in the map leaves me and I say, "I think your bath is overflowing." You rush back inside and I follow.

"It won't stop," you say. And at first I think you mean the water. You are not American. You speak in English but your accent is thick with the dregs of something Eastern European. It's almost as if you were expecting me. You don't ask why I was watching you. I feel as though this whole scene was set for me, an invitation to be part of something bigger. Bigger than my lack of reason for being here in the first place. Or perhaps *this* is the reason. It could be, I think to myself. Why not?

I close the door quietly behind me. Something tells me that we mustn't draw attention to ourselves. Already we've each become something else. Something double. I no longer feel like a fraction of a thing. It only took a moment to create a perfect number.

I see the problem. Without a word you grab her arms and I take her ankles and together we haul the girl out of the bath. I turn off the taps and pull out the plug. The water is cold and pink. Blood slides from the lacerations like oil. It smears the skin, it keeps on sliding. Onto the tiles, onto our clothes, our hands. You run your fingers through your hair and leave a smudge of red on your forehead. "It just won't stop."

There is a *lot* of blood here. I haven't seen so much blood since Kelly was bitten in the face by Sandy. Her lip just split in two. Although her cheeks were punctured, it was that lip, burst like a cherry, that made me feel faint. There's always a lot of blood in the soft parts. The inside of the nose, the lips, the anus. They bleed so easily.

I grab the towel from the rail. It might have been a white fluffy thing once, soft and clean. Now it is rough to the touch and a little yellow. As I press it to the wounds it soaks up the blood like a sponge, mimics the dead girl with its flashes of hard white and moist red. You gasp, "What are you doing?" and yank the towel from my hands. "Look at it. Look." Your voice trembles. "We can't leave the towels like this. What are you thinking?" I grab it back out of your hands and spread it over the girl's face. I'm sick of her glazed eyes looking at me. Accusing me. I crawl over to you, feeling the wetness of blood soak into the knees of my jeans. I take your face in my hands and gently kiss you. Your eyes are wet with tears. Your lips are dry with the heat.

"It's okay," I say, and you nod, like a child. I want to chastise you, but you meant no harm. "I'm here now. Everything will be okay." I hold you close and rock you slightly. You put your arms around me and sob into my shoulder. Yes, everything is going to be fine.

Snake

The flotsam and jetsam of insectacentric circles spelling out precious words on the wall. Murder and blood. They will feast tonight. The net hangs in tatters, a yellowing screen, the smoke and mirrors of an illusionist's den.

Flickering candle flames provide extra heat in this already searing night, a yellow honey glow stretching, but not quite reaching, into the corners. Her long dark legs snake-like, forked-tongue toes hurtling towards the foot of the bed. White material wrapped around her body like the beginnings of a shed skin, stopping short at both collar bone and thigh.

Here's a secret only she and the insects share. Antennae to wingtip they chalk up misspelled vagaries and words on walls, a graffiti historicity. A short life story in blood-filled sacs and transparent wings. Death and solicitude. An ending before a beginning.

When Rosario hears the knock at the door, three quick raps, her toes curl and her thighs open to breathe. Her lips do the same, emitting the slightest rasp of a soul, the fuzzy dark outline of a life soon to be extinguished.

She listens as he lets himself in. He'd never been here before but had told her via the feathered and the finned to leave the door unlocked. He would be her only visitor, and he would knock before entering the carnal den. She couldn't have gone against his wishes had she wanted to, such was the strength of his reason.

Her mother isn't here. Her lover is long gone. Nobody knows. Nobody would have interfered anyway. Not even her sister, from whom she'd begged the money without explanation. Better to say nothing than to lie. A dirty bundle of notes beside the bed, folded and bagged like a grub cocooned.

Through the bedroom door he comes. All black skin and white eyeballs. A tall hat forcing him to stoop through the doorway. This is no Uriah Heep. This is a god. This is Kali's destructive counterpart, with many fingers in many bloody pies. It is all in his posture, his body language, his lips spread wide into a smile. In one hand he holds a medicine bag. His other flitters a language in the air and the harpies crawl away from their words and revert back to insignificant little insects.

Two nurses enter the room. Buxom women each one twice the width and half the height of the man. They wear medical white, a sterile contrast to the bright feathers and clawed bird feet attached to the doctor's garment.

"Rosario?" His voice is deep and throbbing, foreign. "Did you pray?"

His tongue slides loosely around his mouth as he talks, as though he cannot control the fat pink leech.

The heat is rising. Or the air is falling, swirling around table legs and bulging ankles like a hot, wet fog. The sweat lies in patches on Rosario's body. She shakes her head. She knows nothing of any prayer she's supposed to say.

"Do you have the money?" he asks.

Rosario nods and he extends an arm to take the bundle in his hands, rifling through the notes before throwing them in his bag, a Tarot deck, all bearing different faces. Death's head. Hangman's noose. A change is in the air. The doctor reeks of it.

Rosario is small. She might be a paying customer but his gaze makes her feel like vermin. A parasite. He might enjoy his job. But that doesn't mean he doesn't feel superior. She is afraid. Totally in the dark. How will things proceed? Will there be pain? Blood? It was an accident in the first place. But this part is planned, paid for. She is unable to ask questions because no words will heave their way through the dry corridor of her throat. Barely able to move her limbs she is pinned to the bed. Totally alone with these strangers and their charms and curses. She lies

64

sunk into the mattress and feels anaesthetized; the paralysis beginning at her core and working its way outwards.

The nurses come and stand beside her, one on either side of her head, like chakras. An extension of her self.

"We need to pray, Rosario," says the doctor. "This will not be a murder scene." He is rooting in his bag, the splintered sounds of plastic and metal colliding. Rosario's heart beats painfully fast.

"We need to pray for the little one's soul. We need to save him from damnation." From his bag he produces a skinny red snake that hangs limply from his fist like a length of rope. Rosario shrieks. Finds the strength in her arms and legs and begins to thrash. The snake joins in the dance, bending and curling its body to the doctor's music. He soothes it with whispered nothings and it stills its body once more. But Rosario cannot be calmed. There is only one place she can think of where that snake might go and she won't have it. She won't allow that violation. She twists and turns in her bed like a rabbit in a trap but the nurses have their sweaty fists on her, burning her skin where it recoils from their grasp. They prise apart her legs and hold down her arms leaving her mouth free to gape and her eyes to bulge.

The doctor's tongue sticks out like an arrow and then flattens itself against the snake's tail. From there it travels up the length of the body, over glistening red scales up to the diamond-shaped head. He starts a mantra and looks over the girl on the bed, rolls his eyes, rolls his tongue, gestures at Rosario to repeat. The words are difficult to get her mouth around, no more than clicks and animal sounds. Her teeth bite against the words like lumps of plastic. But she tries her hardest because he is coming towards her with the snake, and the feathers on his cloak are rustling and the insects are marching again. He brings both hands over her body, one holding the snake, the other empty and palm-flat against the vibrations emanating from her. He doesn't touch her. He brings the snake up between her legs where she is naked and open and for a moment he lets the tongue flick out and touch her skin while Rosario grits her teeth around the prayer.

65

Then the snake and the man are advancing, up over her stomach, her breasts, to her throat.

Silence. A hard black hand shoots out and pinches her nose. He doesn't speak. The snake watches through black beads. Her nose hurts, he twists his fingers. She opens her mouth to breathe and hands are clamping her jaws. Fat fists hold open her mouth and saliva pools from the corners. The snake head is inside the dark red of her mouth. Her tongue can't escape its roots and she feels the sharp sting of two fangs penetrating the wet pink flesh.

Her body lightens almost immediately; her tongue feels fat and her lips tingle not unpleasantly. He loosens his grip on her nose and she breathes deeply through widening nostrils. Her arms and legs flop lead-heavy onto the bed. The nurses step forward one more time to pry her legs apart and splay her angled on the bed, and then retreat into the dark corners.

Rosario doesn't care. She feels a glow around her, a euphoria. She's addled. Brain-tied, tongue-puckered and lazy. She waits. The snake is back inside the bag. The doctor's hand is rooting again, plucking this and that. And when he brings out the large metal rod and begins to screw a barbed hook onto its end with a careful eye, the insects begin to gather, hungry, to wait for the first drops of blood.

The Pleasure Principle

The air is damp with the scent of semen both fresh and stale. In the corner, a man has dismantled a wooden chair and splinters protrude from between his bloody teeth. A purple-faced man masturbates furiously beside you, the veins in his arm standing out like cord, his penis red and raw like a dog's. You watch two men curled up like babies, sucking on each other and think about joining in, even though you aren't attracted to men in the slightest. You just want the feel of a warm wet orifice around you. But you wouldn't dare go and slip yourself inside a free space in case one of the men attack you. It's been like this for days. You are the newest addition to the ward, but they have paid you no attention. They are too wrapped up in their fantasies. You realise you've all been left alone to fuck and fight each other to the death if necessary. You are the rejects, the abnormalities, the unfortunate users of the black-market Aphrodizia.

It started as a plaything, the Empath-e-kit. A toy for the rich, for the famous. A minor operation to insert a chip into the grey matter for a few thousand pounds, the initial hook up, tubes, wires, questions, data-input, and then left to free-base.

Don't you wish you could experience what you see on the screen?

That's what the ad said. The porn stars with their muscles ready-relaxed, their noses full of junk, you could have that perfect sex experience with the beautiful people. The giant cocks and the gravity-defying tits could be yours over and over for a price. Insert your favourite DVD, lie back and watch as genitals, breasts, lips, tongues, teeth, elbows, the backs of knees, the silky thighs, the six-packs, the tanned flesh come together to pleasure YOU.

Physically safe, emotionally flat-lining, you can play your films on the ceiling of your home, feel the shudder of a woman as she climaxes with you, taste the semen as it spurts into your mouth, feel an accommodating anus around your cock, or the splash of urine warm on your chest. . .

Celebrities made it cool. This wasn't some behind-closed-doors thing. This was fashionable, the way drug use became fashionable and the way anorexia became fashionable. It was sold as the perfect recreational device: fun, safe and socially unacceptable in the most acceptable way.

But not everyone is interested in 'normal', safe, hetero- or homo-sexual sex. There was, of course, a niche in the Empath-e market for the perverse, and it found its way onto the black market, under the name Aphrodizia. For those of you who like your partners a little bit younger, a little bit obese, a little bit anorexic, a little bit ill. . . open wounds, physically disabilities, the over-80s, execution and mutilation. . .

Want to experience your own death?
Want to witness your lover die right in front of you?

There really was something for everyone. Unfortunately you were one of those perverts weren't you. You had your peccadilloes and forked out the couple of hundred to get hooked up.

Totally safe.

Safe as houses, they said.

And it seemed to be both good and true. Until a sudden increase in anti-social behaviour hit the news: harassment, abuse, groping, biting, licking strangers in the street, flashing, masturbating in public, violence, suicide, mutilation and finally murder. Men tried to sever their own cocks, women injured themselves by forcing in kitchen implements, garden equipment and anything else they could get their hands on. Anything to scratch that already-suppurating wound.

The word 'malfunction' started to drip randomly into conversation. It turned out the Aphrodizia chip retained all memories of all the films, the feelings, the whole gamut, while the original Empath-e-kit erased all data between each viewing. So a man might suddenly find himself going rodeo with a beautiful blonde just as he steps out into the road, shooting his load as the car shoots him along the tarmac. Women become Theresas, lost in an eternal ecstasy, forgetting to feed the baby, the dog and themselves, until mind and body are wasted to nothing. Then they are all scooped up and locked up.

There is some talk here, in stolen moments of lucidity, of conspiracy theories. Hell bent on finding an answer, the patients' discussions become heated arguments, become fist fights. Either that or the conversation is halted for the need to empty one's balls of fluid. Most seem to agree it was the government's attempt to clear the streets of the poor and the perverted; the perverted poor. Slip in the bait and then hit them with a double whammy. Maybe, maybe not. Either way, you're here and no one knows. You may as well be dead. Not that anyone cares anyway. You did, after all, kill your girlfriend in a moment of Aphrodizia-rage. And now you're just a number on a graph, a figure on a chart, living the memory over and over again.

Will Travel

His hand smells of hospital soap. A synthetic sterility to mask the stink of germs, disease, bodily expulsions. I would prefer the scent of sweat or grime to this but I am not one to choose. That is half the pleasure, being forced to accept what one is given, under the limited circumstances. It is his left hand and my mouth is level with the place where his knuckles pale as he grips the metal rail in front of me. The larger percentage of him is immediately behind me. I can feel the shape and weight of a body pressing against my buttocks and I know it is his. His corporeality is a series of imprints in the hollow of my back, my legs, my shoulders. There are tiny hairs on his fingers that I want to graze with my lips. I squeeze my thighs together as he pushes against me, a slew of bodies cramming onto the carriage. I hold my breath, my cheeks are warm.

Any moment. . .

I am intent on my subtlety. If anyone were to notice me, were to watch for even a few seconds, they would think me too hot, a little faint from the heat. A little saddened maybe. Lost in daydreams. I bite my lip, and then I breathe. Sharp. Sweet. Breaths. Through my nose. His fingers are so close to my face I can feel the heat coming off them and the sweat from his body now overpowering the sterility, reaching towards me.

There.

Oh the sweetest feeling as I grip the rail myself and look at his hand, the sickle-moon scar on the middle finger on which I could just suck.

Now.

But that would be to end the thing, to finalise the moment, and there is nothing more disappointing than climax.

I am well-practised in this. Not that I chose to unravel my days in this way. Things just happened, as they do, and one day I found the obtuse reasoning behind my need for travel. I have been on the London tube, round in loops on the Tokyo Yamanote Line and the inner and outer circle of the Glasgow subway. I have been transported on buses and trains around France. And yes, I have travelled by plane and by boat. For years I had thought this an instinct for flight, or escape, never feeling quite happy in one town, or even staying in any one building for too long. I was fired from one job for not turning up because I was busy strolling around a city miles away. I have walked out on others because I could no longer stand the thought of staring at a monitor, standing behind a counter or sitting in a classroom surrounded by tiny people cross-legged on the floor. I am a teacher. I have taught. But it just leaves me with a feeling of emptiness.

It was a few years after I moved to Paris that it occurred to me that my movements were developing a pattern of their own. I started to use the metro more than any other form of transport, and then I was becoming more selective over which trains to use. Forget any that go above ground. My trips to St. Ouen soon stopped, though I had enjoyed the dense smells and textures of the flea-market there. I needed to stay beneath the town. The darkest dark and the illuminated yellow, the smothering heat and shallow breaths. I took to travelling in circles around the city centre, charmed by this tubular city existing beneath the other, larger one above, until I finally realised it wasn't my destination that was important.

For a while I thought perhaps it was the stations themselves. The jostling, noisy crowds like cattle, the late-comers running down the escalators, the spiral staircase at Abesses with its painted walls, the chrome interior of Arts et Métiers, the stalls, the woman who brought her keyboard with her to Châtelet everyday and sang along out of tune, the rhythm of the drums, the shouts and yells, even the excitement of an occasional purse-snatch or suicide.

We slow to a stop, the sound of the doors, the push of the crowd to get off, the squeeze of the next body of people. He is still behind me, his hand still wrapped around the pole. He is tight next to me. And he has an erection. It presses into me; I press back in response and then it curves around me and it is not his penis after all. It is his hand. It is flat-palmed on my arse, against my skirt. I am as still as I can be. I can feel the sweat on the back of my neck and between my breasts. His hand moves slowly around me and then presses into the cleft between my buttocks, and rests there. My belly twinges and rocks. I am a series of electric currents that meet between my legs. He is in my most personal place. The satin fabric of my skirt and the cotton of my underwear are the only things between my skin and his. His fingers begin to caress me. The tip of his finger is rubbing against my arsehole. I think I might pass out with wanting him. I feel such a desire to stand with my feet further apart, to invite him in. Yet even if I had the nerve I am totally trapped against the edge of a seat and the people around me. I want to lick his hand, but this isn't the way it should happen. After all these years, I am used to a sexual contact more imagined than real.

Timing is essential. A too-empty train will mean seats for all. No pushing or shoving, no physical contact, just a polite reserve of empty space. Weekends and between the hours of ten and four mid-week are no good. These are full of women hell-bent on shopping to death and tourists just hell-bent. Too absent minded to notice me, they are thinking only of their next excursion.

Often, all *too* often, a homeless person will wander on. They will stand at the front of the carriage and wax philosophical about their situation, their hunger, their children, their inability to find work. Then they will traipse down the aisle with their hands held out. Sometimes, those unwilling or unable to speak will slip a piece of paper onto the knee of each passenger, their speech written instead of spoken, and then make their way back up the carriage, collecting the scraps and, if they are lucky, some loose change. The locals look at them with distaste or tell them to fuck off. Only the tourists are willing to hand out their money.

Sometimes a 'musician' will get on to the train. Like me they spend all day in transit. Hopping from one train to another, knowing how to beat the system, how to avoid paying. They make a racket and are the worst for emptying any train carriage. But they come on only at certain times. I've learned how to avoid them.

Today I disembark at Madeleine. I had planned to go right on to Porte de la Chapelle, through Pigalle, but the daring of my fellow traveller has me feeling queasy. I am in a spin. I push my way through the crowds onto the platform, into the light of the station. I know all these lines, all these stations, like the creases in my own grubby and metallic-scented hand, which is sweating now as I find myself on the street.

Paris is never quiet. There are always people on the streets, no matter what the time. Unlike other cities it breathes life into its inhabitants rather than the other way round, it colours them, changes them to suit itself, moulds them like a surrogate mother. And at any given moment it can neglect them. Crime is plentiful and homelessness rife, but I have never felt afraid. Just a little overwhelmed at the openness. Despite the way the buildings nudge each other and close in onto the streets, it always seems like a universe away from the push and pull of the metro.

The metro. The users. There is my pleasure, my forbidden fruit. Sometimes, I barely have to touch them. To be so close as to feel the hair on my arm touch the fabric on the sleeve of the man or woman sitting beside me can cause such a force of feeling that it shocked me at first. A hand on a knee so close to my own can create a life in me I hadn't known existed before. Though the act itself is far from sexual, I am filled with desire to fill myself, to fuck, and knowing I am going through these motions in secret only drives me further to the brink.

It happens when I am mere footsteps from my front door. I know, instinctively, that the hand on my mouth will have a sickle-moon scar on its middle finger. I know the other around my waist has already touched me, just minutes before. I try to make a noise but the muffled yelp dies away. I thrash about but he is stronger and he pulls me backwards, my feet almost leaving the floor. My heart thuds heavily like a train pounding the track. My legs tremble uncontrollably. A space between two buildings, a dark corridor like something from a dream. My only thought is of murder. Those hands, broad hands, thick fingers with wide flat nails. Those hands I feel I know already. They've become a murderer's tools. They will close around my throat, or beat me to a bloody pulp. They will cut off my oxygen or break my limbs, they will tether me and then peel back my layers. They are all over me, three or four or five hands, tugging at my clothes, pushing me against brick. Pressing, nudging, feeling, groping, imprinting, invading, penetrating. His mouth is wet, banging against mine. He is smudging me, spreading me thin, his knees pushing apart my legs, all the better to find a hole to bury himself in. His eyes are dark and lifeless. The knife blade flashes once in the glow of a street lamp before I feel the tip of it prick at my throat. He says nothing. He knows I won't scream. I am falling inside him. He lifts my skirt and bruises my thighs, feeling his way, seeing with his fingertips. And when they find me slick, when he pushes them inside and I catch my breath, his eyes flash momentarily. And then he punches me and I fall to the floor unconscious.

It is still dark when I wake. It's a heavy dark, comforting like a blanket, hiding me as I lie on cobblestone, sprawled in torn clothes, underwear missing and blood pooled beneath me. I hurt in every place. My jaw feels thick, my left eye is jammed shut and my hands feel like the fingernails have been ripped out, broken off, splintered. I don't dare look. I lift myself vertical and shrink to child-size. I don't know the name of this street, but everywhere leads to the centre in Paris. All lines are umbilical. Just as below ground you can always find your way back so, too, do the streets of the city always take you to the beginning. Past the debris of smashed glass and the burnt out shell of a car, I make my secret way home and nurse my wounds.

Transference, I think, as I look at myself reflected in the passengers' faces. Am I so different from the rest of them? I see a girl of 10 or 11, sitting like a whore. She's a pre-slut, a nymph. She breaks her gaze for no one, just sits with one arm stretched out along the back of the seat while her mother, opposite, yaks on her phone. Behind her, the man's face is lined with creases, sharp, painful, yet tender lines around his eyes and mouth. He chews the stub of an unlit cigar and his yellow fingers curl around a paperback. The suited man with the laptop, the old woman with crooked, arthritic hands, the straggle-haired girl with the drooling dog. When they catch my gaze, they look away quickly, unnerved, perhaps, by the purple bruise on my face. It's my mark, it's the touch of something, by someone, who stole time, and pain and consciousness. But who left me with so much in return. I look at everyone who gets on, everyone who pushes against me. I push back, I angle myself, bend my knee, roll my hips, slide my body into their spaces, the palms of their hands. I take and take and take and fill myself on them, drink their effluence. And still I wait, as the train takes me beyond the dark. I will travel, if only to see him once more.

Birth Control

He pinched me. Right from under my boyfriend's beak. Right from behind a short misanthrope who was holding up the queue in Kwik Save.

I always knew he'd come.

I'd been waiting, waiting to be saved from a relationship that was all pain and no glory.

It was love at first slight. We were all hearts and flowers, take-aways and television. We ached for the feel of one another inside as though we'd never known loneliness before. He craved a second heartbeat, I an extra appendage. For those first few days we lived in harmony, but it couldn't last. Existence is more than a tally of romantic endeavours and licking the Marmite from each other. It was when we moved into a house together that we stopped crossing paths. The rooms were so small we had to take it in turns to shimmy across the floor, timing our manoeuvres perfectly to avoid a collision. Eventually, we had no choice but to divide up the house.

Being a gentleman of a kind he gave me first dibs. I had the choice of a rock or a hard place. After some small consideration I chose the bedroom with its threadbare carpet and peeling wallpaper. That way I knew sleep was always just one level of consciousness away. He claimed the lounge and sat for hours watching the TV that wasn't there, biting his toenails and picking crumbs from his beard. In a moment of territorial largesse he planted his flag in the shag pile and pissed in the four corners of the room as the first snows of winter fell.

We had promised to cover the earth in roses for each other. But this soon dwindled to a bunch of dandelion stalks wrapped in remorse after another argument under a too-low roof. The squeeze was tight. It penetrated right through to the bones. And then I was pregnant and what started as a craving for rawhide turned into a urine-riddled rabbit.

"It's true," I told him. "The doc confirmed it. He said I'm Keith Cheggers alright."

We fought over how it had happened. It can only have been during a sidling past one another in the moist corridor of a two-dimensional room. In a moment, perhaps, of lust and exquisite craftsmanship of opportunity. Love without awareness. Sex without feeling. Perfunctory. Or as a lubricant to ease the once-so-simple act of getting from one side of a room to the other.

We didn't rejoice. This was a new thing on me. I always knew I had a body made for two, but not like this. Not up the junction and no two-ways about it. And boy, what a family we were going to make: mange-eaten, flea-bitten, mould-ridden, pus-stricken. We fed off wood lice and fag ends just to make our two ends meet. And meet they did, usually against the greasy cooker or in the grey-stained confines of a once-white bath. It was the only way to stop the noise of his wheezy breathing and senseless talking. Shut him up with kisses; with cunt; with fingers and gags and odd-shaped pieces of fruit.

For a while we settled into a cacophonous routine, a sly acceptance of the changes to come. He was openly enthralled at every evidence of life inside, every kick and wriggle. He began to talk in hushed tones, as though the baby's ears might be sensitive to the sonic boom of his sweet-talk. He touched me in a new way, his fingers engaged in a more gentle battle with my flesh. There was a kind of tenderness. I was no longer left bruised. And I grew. Bigger.

I was almost happy then, smoking cigar butts as I rocked in the crippled chair, rubbing my yellow paws over the taut drum of my belly. A hard knock of whisky twice a day staved off the morning sickness and hair of the dog-gone kept hangovers at bay.

Happy times. We were broke but he got a job at pest control. I told him to start in the corners of our flat but he was afraid that once

77

caught in the spider webs he'd never be free. He thought arachnids were the souls of women scorned who sought to wreak their petty revenge on him. Such was the burden of his conscience from a previous life. I didn't mind. Their prey came in useful for food, especially when I was eating for two. I was so hungry all the time I thought I might be eating for four and twenty. I filled my face with everything that moved and much that was still. I gathered the weeds from the cracks in the pavement and grazed on them for hours. I nibbled on carpet fibres and dust motes and the blackened crumbs from inside the toaster. I ate things with two legs, six legs, eight legs and four, becoming pest controller in my own home in a perfect Malthusian variant.

I expanded till I could no longer see my feet. My splintering skin retorted with the spelling of a Cyrillic-like text across my abdomen in purple slivers. I was getting ready.

When the time came I struggled to expel. Like drowning. I wanted to inhale the whole atmosphere but all I could do was whistle through my teeth to hail a passing taxi. It refused to stop for a woman labouring. Besides, I was bound. They had forced my legs apart, pulled until my hips dislocated. Tied my ankles to the mast of the ship and pushed me out to sea, water cresting and the seagulls pecking at the flesh. Ripping pieces of my meat and fighting amongst themselves over the bloody red scraps.

It took days. It could have taken weeks. Time was not a continuum but an irregular series of stops and starts interspersed with dreams. Then finally it was over. And as the midwife showed me the fruits of my labour I could hardly believe what a crop she had gathered. Not one, not two, but five little boy tykes before me. Long of face and fair of fur. Five open, toothy mouths wanting to be filled. Newborn crying amplified. It would be a struggle, but I knew I would cope. I fell in love with their dewy eyes and perky ears and I knew we would be fine. I even loved the way they clambered over my body in a race to the breast, leaving bruises from hard hooves and nearly biting off my nipples in their enthusiasm.

But on returning home with my brood, I found things more difficult than I had anticipated. He became a stranger: stranger than before. The children wouldn't bond with him. They pissed in his corners and he felt emasculated. They would end up castrating him, he said. "They're a nuisance." He was sure that one day they would pin him down and steal his manhood as he slept.

"You have no coping mechanism," I said. "You're tired and frustrated and your ego is afraid of the stallions they will grow up to be. But mostly, you're paranoid."

He didn't listen. He just responded in new ways. As the volume of the boys' crying increased, so too did his need for control. No beast was safe. He would gather up his implements, his poisons and his bait and go out in search of prey. Ants were at risk. So too were roaches, lice, slugs, frogs. He moved onto squirrels and pigeons and eventually wound up putting a stray dog or two out of his misery. They all ended up in the same place, buried in the garden by the crotchety old tree.

But it went too far. He was the dysfunctional component in our barely-functioning family. He was upsetting the children and soon they refused to feed.

"Look at what you've done with your crazy behaviour," I yelled. "Be a man," I said, "and deal with it."

He seemed genuinely shocked. "It's got nothing to do with me, bitch. It's you. Your milk's gone sour."

It hit me hard. His tone, his anger, the realization. Of course, that pungent odour I had recently noticed but barely acknowledged. I was so used to the rancid smells that filtered through the house that it hadn't occurred to me that something might be amiss. How repulsive, my body in the throes of betrayal.

I had to get out of the house. I wanted the symmetry of the outdoors, the open air and calm expanse of space, squeezed though it was between walls. Maybe that's it, I thought. Maybe it's getting to me too, the constant stench of effluvium.

But that's when I realized the smell had gone. I'd walked for hours. I'd listened to the sounds of the street and I'd questioned my own worth and only then did it hit me. The smell had gone; the bastard had lied. My milk had not turned. That stink, that stench could only be one thing – the perfume of his wretched self-loathing.

I arrived home, if a place that bred such hatred could be called home. There was not a sound. I switched on the light and knew immediately that something was not right. Where were the roaches scuttling into the dark corners? Where was the sound of tiny hooves stampeding on the linoleum? The floor was littered with the bodies of bugs under carapace, some upside down with legs drawn. It was a plague of dead insects. Here a rat with blood spilling in a tight little pool, there a mound of snail shells with occupants dried to a crust. And there, at the furthest end of the room sat my brood in a nervous huddle, twenty shit-matted legs entwined in a millipede fashion. They wouldn't look at me. No, they couldn't take their eyes off the bigger mound on the kitchen floor. The large he-shaped bundle of purple flesh, all hoof-indented. He looked like he'd been hit by a truck. I looked from the five to the one, saw the vomit dripping from their lips and knew. There had been a battle. His pest-control had gone too far. But they had won. They had emasculated him, as he'd said they would. And it didn't matter. I had five boys, I didn't need this one toxic freak, poisoning our family unit.

And that smell, that stench that wasn't sour milk after all, would soon dissipate, once he was six feet under with the rotting cream of his murdered crop.

Penny Whistle

I've been the glamorous girl. Been the envy of the little girls with stars in their eyes. Been the bird gliding through the air, feathers on my rump and in my cap, born to catch that swing in the crook of a bent knee, an outstretched hand, a muscley thigh. I've had my glory days; the trapeze girl in all her glitter. Relishing the ooohs and aaaahs, lifting the audience to my dizzy heights, giving them a catalogue of near-deaths and a hero's incredible save night after night.

I've been the blond angel, winking at my partner as we pass in the rafters, in our own world, smiling smiling smiling. They queued up to be with me. The knife-thrower, the lion tamer, the sword-swallower, the fire-eater. I had them all. They left me empty, even with their toys and their unique gifts.

They couldn't throw me out. They couldn't leave behind the girl who had been born in the circus. Oh, they tried. They upped and left. Packed up the animals, the swords, the tight and slack ropes, the big top, and took off. Leaving me drunk and oblivious, hungover and sore. But I can't stand to be alone. I need to be surrounded by the noise and the scent of animal sweat, the promise of danger, the booming voices. So I found them. It wasn't difficult. It took me two weeks. Robbie and I hitched lifts. Not many cars will pick up a girl and her dog. There would have been even less if they'd seen what I am like from the neck down. It's my insides seeping out I would tell them. Part of me was waiting for my beautiful abductor. Part of me wanted the rape and murder tale. Part of me wanted a somewhat fit ending to my life.

They didn't want a crippled girl. A has-been beautiful girl.

Now I am withered. I'm crooked and bright pink. My scars turn to red hot when I'm angry. They glow like I'm still aflame. But they had to honour my mother, Daria. She was a brilliant rider, apparently. I've only seen the photos: standing tall on a wide-backed black horse as it galloped in circles; balancing on one foot, toes clenched, leg-muscles pinched. I was born to them. I was her gift. They couldn't just throw me away, even after the fire rendered me ugly and useless.

I drink to ease the pain. Burnt skin never ceases to crack and weep. I sleep on my left side. I wear loose clothes and rub cold creams into the creases. Sometimes I rub butter in. It doesn't do any good in the long run but it's a temporary relief. Especially when Robbie licks it off. The soft rhythmic rub of his warm tongue is very soothing and sometimes I think he knows it helps. He enjoys the taste but, more than this, I feel he understands my sighs. Once or twice, or three times, when I have been almost to the point of passing out drunk, I have rubbed the butter between my legs and cried when his tongue made me sway my hips despite myself.

The clowns make me laugh. Whenever I can I watch them rehearse. I don't like to be there during their actual performances because I can't stand the crowds, the people who once loved me. The very same who would now cover their children's eyes if they ever saw my naked body. Arnie, Bluey, Harry and Marvin have been with the circus at least as long as I have. Their avuncular nose-pinching and raspberry-blowing had me crying with laughter as a child. And now as a twenty-year old woman they come round to my trailer in the dead of night, a response to my weeping, and entertain me with their band of miniature instruments. A tiny toy plastic piano, a broken banjo and penny whistle. Sometimes I sing with them. My voice isn't good. But neither is it that bad and singing lets out a whole lot of steam. It was Arnie who named me Penny after seeing my new act for the first time.

Yes, I am useful again. No longer redundant. I have my uses. Fuck my mother's honour. They didn't really give a shit about that. When they realised I had talent as a trapeze artist, Frank was hell-bent on keeping me there, never mind my age. Once I was disfigured, he couldn't wait to be rid of me. It took some quick-thinking on my part to land myself a new job. Something perfect and, as it turned out, very profitable. Once I'd caught up with them the last time they left me behind, I went to Frank with my plan. He never tried to abandon me again.

Adult entertainment. Live flesh. Leave the animals for the children. What I suggested, in a different tent, with a door-man-cum-security, was women. Naked women. Stripping women. Dancing women. Not hour-glass beautiful but uniquely attractive women. Here would be something different for an audience with a more refined taste. Here we would have the painted ladies, the twins, the obese, the bearded, the dwarves... the crippled. It was an immediate success.

I could never quite figure out why the clowns gave me so much joy. Perhaps it was the sadist in me who enjoyed to see another person's misfortune, be it a custard pie in the face or a rubber hammer to the back of the head. Perhaps it was my relief from the constant working: training, exercising, balancing, swinging. They would make me laugh so hard my stomach would ache for days afterwards.

Last month, Harry lost his fight against cancer of the liver, hard on the moonshine right up to his final hours. We held a grand funeral and buried him by the side of the river in his hometown, the place he would sit for hours and dream up new pranks. He was a huge Harry Lloyd fan, as was his father, who had named him after the comedian. In his place we got Danny, a handsome young twenty-something. There were so many wannabes at the audition. Queues of clowns. Red noses, white faces, happy faces, sad faces, huge feet, big trousers, fuzzy wigs. A constant chatter. A fluttering, squeaking, clattering . . . barking dogs, costumed-dogs, balloon dogs. But in the end, whatever it was they were after, Danny had it and he joined their troupe immediately.

I took a shine to him straight away.

There are some people who love the circus so much they will trail after it, become an entourage. Even though they see the same tricks night after night, they come back time after time, finding huge delight in the season's new performances, excited at the prospect of being the first witness. Often they will help out behind the scenes, the circus having all the glamour of rock and roll to those from the outside.

I had my regulars and my suitors when I was 'Angel' the trapeze girl. I don't have so many now. In fact, I think I have only one. One man who I began to notice about three months ago. A man with thick black hair and soft kind eyes. He came every night. He sat in the tent and came to almost every show. There were three a night and if he was there for one, he was there for all. He sat in the same place if it wasn't too busy, right at the front, for the best view. Here I was Penny Whistle. Here I was Pierrot. Here I was right. A clown, a cripple and a slut. All of those offensive terms and more. Every night he would hold my gaze as the band played and I began to shed my clothes. He didn't join in the gasps as the wretched pink criss-crosses over my body were slowly exposed. He didn't lean forward with the rest of the audience who tried to make sense of me, to find the womanly curves, the small rounded tits missing the punctuation of nipples, the pubis without its hair. Sometimes he would smile, and it wasn't out of sympathy like the others who often caught sight of me outside. He was attracted to me in some strange animalistic way, and when I did my whistle act he remained silent as the others cheered and clapped.

It was never quite enough though, this attraction. There were still jeers and hoots and terrible, terrible insults. More than once I ran off the stage screaming. The physical and emotional pain was often unbearable. But it was all I had left and I was the star of the freak-show, winning over more audiences, in one way or another, than the conjoined twins and the mermaid girl put together, whose shows were much more erotic than my own. There was nothing subtle in my show. There was myself, my body, and the music I made.

So the clowns would come and entertain me. They dried my tears with handkerchiefs pulled from sleeves or let me cry on the worn shoulders of their too-big overcoats. And then one night when dawn was teasing the horizon they left me to sleep beneath the blanket Robbie and I shared. They crept out of the van like thieves and I dreamt of birds without feet and horses with wings and when I awoke, there was Danny, looking down at me, his mouth pulled taut against his painted smile. He drew back the blanket and began to unbutton my shirt. "You are the most beautiful woman I have ever seen," he said, and I did not protest. "I have watched you perform every single night," he said. And when he removed his top hat and his black hair sprung out at odd angles, I looked into his soft kind eyes and saw my admirer. I let him undress me as I had before in my dreams. When he took a pair of handcuffs from his top pocket I lay down still and let him cuff my wrists to the bedposts. As he brought out my walking cane from beneath the bed my breathing shallowed and my body swelled. As he pulled out a string of handkerchiefs from his sleeves I opened my mouth wide to let him stuff them inside. And as he beat me across the face till I bruised and bled, I felt whole and beautiful, and free as a bird.

Still Life

A hunger for flesh desire, but not for taste, because the pleasure does not flower from bud to blossom in the fissure of an open mouth. Neither does it bleed through the pores to lick clean with a dry hooked tongue. It is not found in the whisper of a breath like distant purring, nor the scent of sweat long turned stale. The pleasure, the hunger's satisfaction lies in the sight, the appearance: that exquisite, vulnerable serpent on whose scabrous form the artist will never cease to tread.

Three mirrors to provide three sides of the same face. The lie, the truth, the imagination. Candles melted the air into suspended dusk, drawing the ceiling in tones of pink and yellow, casting an ashen shadow over gauze. A book laid open on a wooden block, the chopping block, with a basket beneath to capture the bloodied scraps. The pages were a manifestation of colour and shadow, makeup, blending, touching up and toning down. Notes and symbols in pencil, words underlined—a subtext written by the artist's hand. Guinevere was the artist. She was the defacer and the self-defaced, the god, the voyeur, the introvert and the exhibitionist. And tonight she was going to try something new.

Creatively mutable and of fertile mind. Hair raked back from clean scrubbed face. A kimono wrapped and fastened tightly around her childish waist. A rapid movement, a flickering of the hand. Eyes pierced their reflection; eyes times eyes times eyes times eyes. In her hands a whisk and a glass bowl, pestle and mortar. She beat the egg white and then rubbed the gluey paste onto her face. An idea stolen straight from the book. She had tried her pancake makeup, moisturisers, foundations, powders. And today had learned of an age old trick for whitening the skin. A natural cosmetic from a plain old chicken egg.

86

Full lips powdered in white, darker in the cracks, like parchment; eyes pastilled in ochre, sunken, shadowed. And now her face was a void, a creamy white mask to conceal the salubrious glow which usually surrounded her like an aureole. She let down her hair, a dark mane that alighted on her shoulders like a flock of birds with feathered feet to grip the flesh. The look had a certain charm, a quality that was more realistic than her previous attempts. Still, it did not really meet expectations. There was charm, yes, but no solid structure, no molecular motion to bring the vision to life. Ha, irony. But isn't that what art stands for? It is irony in its most singular form, a parody, a juxtaposition, a complimentary disagreement, a hybridism. It is black and white in colour, depth in superficiality, love in hate and life in death.

She dropped her kimono and lay, naked, draped on the bed, limbs silken, hair like lace, eyes of velvet agate. Unblinking, tunnel vision, tuned into space, a dead star. Arms open in commandment, legs parted, bestial, folded and scrapped like the victim of a sex crime. The sparse mound of hair below her naval was beaded with sweat and her nipples were erect as though ready to give nutrition. This game always aroused her. It was the tincture of aphrodisia in her exorbitance, her exuberance, her extroversion. In putting on the mask she was erasing her spectral genesis. She was Venus in a death shroud; she was Persephone at the gates of the Underworld. But still it was not right.

She sighed and rolled off the bed, covered her body in silk, sat down and began to scour away her outer skin. Pasted to the mirror and the reflection which presided there were photographs dotted like verse, chorus, verse. Tomes I and II. Pre and post. Pictures of herself, the watcher and the watched. Her face stared out in the same guise over and over. A death pallor that lacked the fruits of cessation. She had not bothered to take a snapshot of today's effort, it would be a waste of a frame.

And there were other pictures. Other girls, other faces, other flesh. These were her guides, her mentors and her work. She had photographed them to retain the image, the perfect moment. Because in reality it would never last.

She showered, slipped on a black lace dress which revealed her perfect shoulder blades and spine. She knotted her hair, stepped into black stilettos. The mirror in the bathroom was steamed up, weeping in condensation; condescension. She wiped it down and painted her lips like a cut. Admired her look, stained her wrists and throat with the perfume of voodoo and then she left the house.

It was an early morning return and she recognised the rich smell as soon as she stepped through the front door. Moist, malodorous, malignant. It was faint, but still she wondered how she could not have noticed it earlier. Smeared lipstick, a saline rim around her lips from the man she had just tasted. Hair ripped down, almost taken from the scalp; bite marks patterned her back and the nape of her neck from a vicious act of love-making. Now all she wanted to do was sleep. Alcohol had drained the energy from her body, her insides permeated with its impure properties. To sleep, to dream. . . But first, the smell. She had to get rid of it. She hated it, that smell of decay.

The bathroom. A rose coloured bath. Candles dotted around the floor had leaked their waxy essence in globules of white and red, her favourite colours. The symbolism of evil good, virgin whore, still life. She knelt before the enamel casing of the bath as though in worship, slipped her fingers into the crack at the edge. When she first moved into this flat she had considered making a complaint to the landlord about this broken, removable piece. And then she had discovered its properties. By some form of magic she had found it to be the perfect storage compartment.

The girl was all bunched up and Guinevere turned her face away in disgust as a sirocco of death perfume ate at her nostrils. She was tucked up in utero, knees up to her chin, feet turned in on one another, hands twisted on brittle wrists, torso ragged and creased. Sea-urchin, waterlogged twists of hair, limbs like tendrils, like left-overs. Rigour mortis had long since departed, leaving in its wake this velvety pulp, soft sand patterns of blissed-out skin. Guinevere grabbed the girl by her rough edges and heaved and the body flopped out like a fish. The artist hated this. She was always cursing herself for leaving it so long. She ought to destroy the body as soon as it had served its purpose.

The girl was disintegrating. Her beauty had faded as beauty does. She had journeyed past the stage of horror-film actress with eyes barely glazed, lips still tinged in pink, body just beginning to cool. This girl's flesh had turned a slight blue, a bitter tangle of veins that felt strange to Guinevere's fingertips. Around her throat a trace of wire was still embedded in the skin, the wire which Guinevere had used to kill her.

In truth it was all mimicry. This one and that one. Guinevere was trying to capture something special, a twin gem, even just an essence, of the girl she had discovered that night in the park. Dead on arrival. Strung out on gravel, bathed in moonlight, starlight, stoned like a statue. Her face serene, smiling like a Mona or a Lisa, fingers closed tightly around a silver cross at her throat, skirt hitched up to reveal thick thighs, long legs, bare feet. Guinevere had studied her closely, this Japanese girl with golden skin and sensual black eyes. Had turned her over, fascinated, like a child trying to find the maker's name. How had the death instinct become so strong? She saw ripped clothes, stones crudely forced into skin, a small pooling of blood. This girl who had jumped from the old bridge was perfect. Guinevere had taken her home.

And now, an aeon later, she had the body of a different girl in her arms, a girl of woad, and still she had not found a trace of that near smile, that serenity. It was the way they died, with fear in their eyes and a scream on their lips that spoiled the effect. Perhaps now she had reached the pinnacle of her creativity. Perhaps finally the artist in Guinevere would merge with the woman. Perhaps tonight things would take a different turn.

She huddled the body quietly into the car and drove away, wine-filled veins pumping their elixir around her body as the exhaust fumes fired the night air with poison.

Even the dark embrace of the grave did not produce a look of surprise from the girl. Festering eyes and open mouth filled with earth, soon to translate into dank bliss for the worms and the maggots. Somewhere around here those blind pink and brown digits would be dancing through the humus and feasting on another six bodies. Ruined, empty, each one a fraction of Guinevere's creative search for the perfect semblance of a Still Life.

It was the title of her current piece of work. She had long since passed the submission date to the gallery but it was not something she could just give up on. It had taken a hold of her mind, expanding and enlarging to destroy all other thought processes. She could not just say goodbye to something so consuming, so intoxicating. And it came to her now that what she had been doing was all wrong, using these girls. It was not remorse she felt, or guilt, it was simply annoyance at a waste of time. As she tore at dead leaves with her shovel, her heels sinking into soft soil, her brow creased with exertion, she knew it was the right and only moment, the only way to get the picture she desired, to make the piece complete. She had everything she needed right here and it was to be the grandest finale ever played out on a live stage.

Her camera, her tool, her melody maker, was in the boot of the car. With hands trembling from the excitement she combed her hair and tucked loose strands into place. She reapplied her lipstick and wiped the dirt from her dress. She darkened her eyebrows and picked the soil from beneath her nails. She was feverish, eager for an epilogue.

The camera had a timing device, all she needed to do was set it to go off in a few seconds. That would be all the time she needed, all the time in the world. She balanced it on the ledge where she sat with her legs dangling, the hem of her black dress pulled taut around her thighs. From where she rested on top of the old bridge she could see the gravel path directly below. The path where she had found her prize one night a lifetime ago. She had no time for thoughts now, no time for last minute thanks, no time for a threnody. She swallowed a final trace of adrenaline-flavoured saliva, and let go.

She hit the ground like a bomb, sending stones flying out like shrapnel, her legs breaking, her head cut, her fingers clutching the ankh around her throat, one shoe on, one shoe off, her eyes calm, her mouth contemplating a smile. . . The camera did not flash. It lay before her, shattered, brought to the ground without a single shot of the most perfect picture of death, a still life.

Sweetmeats

I didn't try to resist the urge to touch it, even when Becky told me to stay away from the filthy, diseased thing. I knew it would be responsive to my fingers, cushioned like a tongue. It had that pale coffee-brown hue that most people hope never to see, and the accompanying sulphuric scent of rot. I recognised it instantly as a kidney; a pig's kidney. Though why it was lying there, tucked away at the side of the road I couldn't begin to guess.

But that wasn't important. When I held my prize up to the light I saw such potential. With the sunlight shining through it, every trajectory from A to B was painted red and I could already see the art I could make with this once-living thing.

I have never shied away from those organic vessels, dead or alive. In fact, my Aunt Ruth has always sworn it was not the gin that knocked me out as a baby, but the smell of blood from my uncle's butcher shop. My mother would take me there when I was turning purple with rage and as soon as she walked through the door my screams would become sniffles. Uncle Bob would take me in his arms and press my tiny body against his bloody apron, much to the horror of the slack-jawed gossips in the queue. With me in the palm of one meaty hand and his knife in the fist of the other, he would continue to chop and, later, as I reached my teens, that motion would feature in my fantasies. The way he handled the meat, the curl of his moustache, the snug fit of his bloodied apron. . .

Back then though, he was my saviour for other reasons, as the only one who could soothe me. I grew up surrounded by the carnage and ungodly slumber of animal cadavers, the reams of white fat, the sweet scent of fresh meat and the rancid stench of shit, and I thought of that shop as my second home My time was spent drawing finger patterns in spilled blood; my imaginary friends were the ghosts of butchered beasts. It was always assumed I would take over my uncle's business when he died, but that thought was far from my mind. I didn't want to sell the meat. I wanted to keep it.

Bob gave me his heart. I know he would have given it freely, had I asked him before he died. So learned am I in the skills of carvery, so dextrous in the art of slicing and dicing, I was able to remove the organ without suspicion. The finest slit left in his chest that might have been one of many cuts made before death. Butchers are always covered in scars. I find it's part of the attraction. He lay there compliant and still, proud, I'm sure, of my meticulous work. He's the one who taught me about precision. He taught me my obsession. I'm sure he would be pleased if he could see his sweet heart now, sitting on my bedside table, a token of my needs.

Foetus

In convex diametrics shiny backed 'roaches criss-crossed the wooden floor and over Heaven's swollen feet. Biting bugs with canine teeth traced their way up her fat calf and bit into the skin, fattening themselves on her blood and tissue, a vampiristic gorging. Occasionally, when taken by surprise, Heaven slapped a sticky palm over the lusty creatures, crushing them against her leg where the corpses would remain for days until they withered and chipped off, as much a part of her by then as an unpicked scab. But usually she allowed them their time, their feed. Who was she to deny a hunger, even of something far less removed than she from Genesis? She was as helpless as these creatures in her gravid state, pregnant, expectant, swollen, her bulging width spread grotesquely in the armchair.

Glass tanks lined the room, home to heterogeneous forms of caterpillar, pupa, butterfly, lava, aphid, moth, other forms of imago. All were writhing and crawling behind glass, feeding on glutinous green, getting fat like Heaven, like calves getting ready for the slaughter. And on the floor insect bodies had turned to dust, depleted of fluid, folded up and shrunken. The pleated paper wings of Cabbage Whites danced around the floor from the breeze that sighed through an open window, and pale brown moths with the soft down of a mouse circled the naked light bulb in frantic worship.

Babies crawled naked over a Tarot card spread and played with a bowl of needles and twine: Zinnia's drug paraphernalia and answers for a Thanatos drenched existence. He sat naked and cross-legged; virile, unwashed and unashamed. His penis thick and opulent, still wet with Heaven's putrefaction. The growth inside her was his doing. She watched from her throne as he picked up a laughing baby and moved it to one side; she watched it come crawling right back. His penis swept the floor as he

94

moved, perhaps picking up dust with its tongue, mites that might cling to the antennae of his pubic hair. Heaven could be one of those bugs. She would find a way inside him, worship him subcutaneously, then she would not have to face his revulsion.

If he should become erect Heaven would heave her way over to him, cradling her mass in her hands. Directed by desire, a masochistic id, she would stretch over him, lower herself onto him, twist and squirm until he found a place to eject his ectoplasm, as he had done once before. As she slept beside her husband in the afternoon of a dirt-grey day Zinnia had crept close beside her. His extended penis had probed her, eaten its way into her through the skin, blackened her with the plague. In the morning she had discovered the child in her womb and her husband Lao had been overjoyed with the result of a divine conception. But that was four days ago and Heaven had not seen him since. And four days ago Ariel had become sick and surrendered his body to another, stronger, entity. Now Heaven wanted Zinnia again. To perfect the infidelity by her rules. But he would not play the game. Because he had created the rules and the fourth day was the day of rest and only he could change that.

"Death," he shouted triumphantly.

"Oh, let me taste your substance," cried Heaven, excited by his sudden realisation.

He looked at her and held up the card of yellow white bones. A forgotten needle protruding from his foot bobbed up and down as he moved, his veins laced deep beneath the skin, blue-black and poisonous.

"You have the Death card."

He crawled to her, let his chin rest on her knees, flicked a cockroach from her thigh.

"Death is good," he said. "Change, transition from one form to another. You will transmogrify."

He swept his hand into the air, cupped his fist around a Red Admiral that had dared to take flight from a safe place, and pulled free a wing like a rose petal. The twitching brown body he threw to the floor; the wing he folded into a neat package.

"Eat," he said and Heaven held out her fat yellowed tongue.

"Here is my body," and the pretty red wing melted into the saliva that poured over Heaven's lips. "The Eucharist," he said. And for wine, for blood, he urinated in her mouth. The toxins made her gums bleed but this was a small sacrifice for the infidelity. Sensation was her only measure of reality. This was his being, this love affair made flesh, made real.

In the corner, Ariel groaned.

The cause of his four-day disintegration was unknown. Even Zinnia could draw no conclusion from the Tarot. His weight had dropped, his skin a paste smeared over his skeleton. Through excessive maceration and the virus that was visibly annihilating him, he was falling through purgatory. Clad in robes that swaddled his thighs and pelvis he lay in the arms of Avarice. He had not moved for four days and Avarice herself was motionless, afraid to breathe lest she cause him more harm. He was a corpse by any definition, a *pietà*—the woman and the body of Christ, before death, before the renascence. But there was hope in Ariel's lungs yet. He coughed up a jet of black liquid and Avarice began to rock him back and forth, his skull resting between her heavy breasts, and the aching heart that shadowed a pulse.

"Come on baby," she breathed into his naked scalp that smelled of milk. His eyes half closed, his temperature beginning to drop.

"You have the world," said Zinnia as he noticed the needle in his foot and slid it free. He looked at Avarice and held up the card.

"It's the end of a cycle, the journey is over sweetheart. Let him go."

Avarice flipped him the middle finger, and then the front door opened.

A blast of rain swept into the room, swirling up tiny insect corpses and displacing them dispassionately. The babies screamed and Lao stood in the doorway, a silhouette in grey faded background, rain dripping from the wide brim of his Stetson.

"Baby, I'm home," he said and went to Heaven's side.

But the shock of his sudden return on her pleasure-seeking body brought on her contractions, and Zinnia smiled wryly in the corner.

Heaven began to surge and retch. Her breathing was an expansion, panting in oxygen, groaning and choking she did not want the baby to come out. She would vomit a suppurating after-birth that she would have to carry around with her for the rest of every life she could afford to inhabit. She grabbed hold of both of Lao's hands, tried to snap his fingers, tried to rip off the claws that extended over twelve inches from each index finger, while he ejected soothing words into her ear. Zinnia was laughing at her side.

The baby wanted to come out. Ariel in the corner began to splutter and Avarice let out a wail, "He's dying." But no one heard because the floor was flooded with embryonic waters. Heaven's legs were hooked around the arms of the chair and, with simian hands raised, Lao was ready to catch the babe. With a chirping Heaven's dilated girth expanded further and as she ejected the tiny body from her huge womb, Ariel heaved up a blood soaked breath and inhaled no more.

The baby was a bird, featherless and pink in Lao's hands. He brought his lips to its frame and kissed its closed eyes. He could lock his hands over the body without crushing it, feel the claws of its feet lining the territory in his hands, his heart and life lines running in parallel. Avarice was weeping but no one cared now, something new had replaced the old; a reversal. Ariel was the imago, the bird was the larva. It was a heart, a bloody pulse in Lao's hands, the ever after, the Resurrection.

And then there was nothing; no sound, no movement, no breath. And Avarice was still. Everyone watched Lao's hands, his face with wide white eyes. Even the crawling babies stopped and watched. And then a miracle. Ariel took a breath.

"Praise the Lord," sang Avarice through gritted teeth. As a non-believer this was torture but she had to admit it was a miraculous recovery and undoubtedly performed by the Lord himself. And then Lao opened his hands. The bird had danced a pretty step. Its death throes had smeared its mantle of Heaven's blood and mucus all over the flesh of Lao's palms. Now it lay in a ball, sticky and pink. A tear splintered down Lao's cheek like brocade, then another. Heaven tried to see but the weight of her exhaustion kept her pinned to the chair. Lao could not allow his beloved to see the dead Lao Junior. Instead he threw it to the babies who pulled off its wings and devoured its corpuscle body.

"No!" screamed Zinnia as he lunged for Lao, "He was my boy." But with lengthened claw Lao injected Zinnia with a presentiment to death, through his body, through his lungs so Zinnia struggled, writhed, stretched and died.

"So, the bird was Zinnia Junior, after all?"

Heaven panted scared and premonitory.

"Harlot," sneered Lao as he climbed out through the window, leaving Heaven to create something from the mess. Leaving her to pick the scars of the birth until a new transformation could heal the flesh.

IIIVVWVVIIIVV

My mother is nothing. My dad is an angel. My sister is Chinese and I always wanted to be her. I dreamed up convoluted ways to kill her—bleach injections for a whiter hide, a drowning with rope-tied hands, a dismantling of her insides squeezed into cat-shaped jars.

I see Jesus watching me every time I come around to these thoughts and he isn't waiting to point the finger. No, he's a voyeur. So I sit in dark circles in our single room and put a whole bunch of keys in my mouth. The hard taste of teeth-jarring metal a risk of asphyxiation, or perhaps just to stop me biting my own tongue. One has to prepare for such things as seizures. One wrist handcuffed to the radiator, the other free to finger my rosary, and my belt buckle doesn't even make a noise as it scratches the surface of the table. Oh my god oh my god oh my god if my sister knew I could see Jesus she would spit blood just to kiss his pinkie.

The small dark-skinned boy who might have been my brother (but who knew, really? Who could tell?) tried to kill me every time you locked me in, mother, with the changing locks and my key didn't fit the hole, it only fit inside the half-circles of my jaw. In the darkness he would traumatise me and try to strangle me until finally I convinced my daddy and he punctured the boy's skull with a single hammer blow. It cracked, split open like chocolate-covered ice-cream. We threw the body into the sea. The edge that lapped at the steps at the end of the garden at the bottom of the house in the green chalky vegetation that was our sunny beach.

But then you, sister, thought you saw Jesus in the back, hiding half out of the foliage, half in the black spots where the moon doesn't quite catch hold. Fingers stiff and pointing right into your insides and the spasms you thought were euphoria or an epiphany. I wanted to teach you what your epiphany was but our mother told me not to be so hurtful. Your epiphanies are as good as anyone else's. So I listened and you were in love with this moronic stranger in the garden. I wanted to tell you what your Jesus does. That he watches me when I fist-fight. Yes. But you don't believe in shadow-boxing and you never listened to my mouth anyway, with its own heartbeat and bloodied belt-buckle smart. I say thank you dad and kill it before it eats itself. I dream of becoming Medea and murdering my own creation so nobody else can take it from me.

The boy's body didn't flow out on the no-tide. The water rose till it kissed our house of ill-repute and no foundations. It rose and rose and the body didn't get carried out to the gulf of Mexico. It just floated outside our back door and smelled of decay and became ashen grey and bloated like a wreck. And then my sister stopped seeing Jesus and we sat together and watched as the birds began to devour him.

Le Café Curieux

1932

She presses a tissue to her lips and stains it bright red, a bow-shaped replica of her mouth. She looks at her eyes in the little mirror, the neatly arched brows, the green and copper irises. Some women would die for a face like hers. She has a face that can stop men in their tracks and a body that could make them cry. Some of them. Others just want to kill her. She looks over at him. He hasn't stopped talking yet. And they say it's women you can't keep quiet. Politics, this Hitler guy, how he's going to get into power some day. What does she care about politics, and foreign politics at that? She sighs, leans back in her chair and looks around. Vern is setting up to play. Already men and women are leaning against the piano, using it as a table for their drinks. Where the hell are Sue and Graham? Late. She turns away from the crowd, the other customers having noisy fun, chatting, playing cards in the corner, singing, laughing. She rests her elbows on the table and looks at Jack. He is staring at her, his mouth closed and his eyes hard. She raises her eyebrows, daring him. But as he opens his mouth to speak the door is thrown open and Graham walks in, smiling. Jack stands and they pat each other on the back. Anna remains seated and lets Graham bend down to kiss her on both cheeks.

"Where is she then? Don't tell me she's not here yet?"

"I thought she was coming with you," Anna says.

"She was here," says Jack. Anna glares at him. "It was when you'd gone to the bar. She sat down, then realised she didn't have any cigarettes, said she was going to run out and get some."

"Well that must have been at least half an hour ago," says Anna. "And why didn't you tell me she was here?"

Jack shrugs and is perhaps about to say something when Vern stops him with a fluttering of the piano keys. A loud cheer follows.

"Can I just say," shouts Graham, "that you're looking charming tonight, my dear."

Anna sneers, turns it into a smile. She stands, straightens her skirt. "Excuse me," she says, with the motion of 'powdering her nose'. Bloody Graham, always trying to make her squirm in public. As if she didn't have enough guilt already, he had to rub it in right under Jack's nose. Knowing full well that if he ever found out. . . well, he'd no doubt blame her as the whore who'd used her wily snake-charm and white thighs to get into Graham's bed. Graham, who remained innocent throughout and would never, ever, fuck his best friend's girl unless forced at gun-point.

The café owner is leaning against the bar, drumming his fingers on the red-painted wood in time to the music. His eyes scan the room constantly, as if he was waiting for someone. He looks shifty. Guilty. Always does. He glances after her as she heads down the stairs to the bathroom.

With one foot on the chair in the ladies room Anna readjusts her stocking, straightening the seam down the back of her leg, whilst the large lady at the sink beside her suddenly bends and closes her fat fingers around something shiny on the floor.

"I think you dropped your necklace dear," she says, holding her palm out. Anna stares at the hand. She can see the sweat gleaming in the heart line, the life line, the nails all tacky red, the name Sue in gold and the place where the chain has snapped.

"Thanks," she says and takes it, careful not to touch the pink flesh. The woman nods and bustles out of the room. And that's when she sees the large red splashes, three perfect circles of blood near the door as it swings shut behind her.

1953

"I had to die 5 times today."

The waiter pauses for just a moment, and she gives him a sweet smile, unlit cigarette clamped between her teeth. He takes a lighter from the top pocket of his shirt and lights her cigarette, service with a smile. He doesn't speak, just goes back to wiping down their plastic table, leaving droplets of water like spittle in the cloth's wake.

"How?"

"Shot in the lung, drowned in my own blood. Gurgled my way through the scene 5 times. Damn Alex. He isn't that great a fucking director, he's just a perfectionist."

"There must be something kind of intimate about having someone shoot you over and over."

Jess's eyes wander over to the Seeburg where a group of men hang around like it's a pretty woman, arms stretched around its sloping body and cigarettes made up mostly of grey ash, hanging permanently from scowling mouths.

Boys.

"I didn't see the killer," she says. "The shot came from the window of an abandoned warehouse. There was no intimacy."

She readjusts her powder-blue cardigan around her shoulders and stares at her friend. She looks ridiculous with all that pink lipstick. It really doesn't suit her. She wonders if she should say something.

"It *can* get kind of chilling though, dying over and over. Die. Cut. Die again. Cut. Again. There are only so many times you can die convincingly before it appears fake."

She looks around. The boys have gone. Peggy Lee blasts out. Single people sit in booths sucking up milkshakes through fat straws, eating fried eggs, reading newspapers. All of them are alone, lonely, making the *Café Curieux Diner* their home from home.

"I'll never understand why you come to this place," says Lorraine, "instead of the Feathers. Isn't that where all your actor friends hang out?"

Jess is silent for a moment and Lorraine wonders if she's heard her. She takes a sip of cola which is warm and almost flat.

"A girl died here, you know." She says, slowly, as though enjoying the tacky texture of the words in her mouth.

"You mean the Hughes girl? I heard they never found a body. They said she's still officially missing. Although I've also heard she was dragged out of the river, all beaten up. It's just a myth, some story made up to get this place some attention."

"She died right here," says Jess, as though she hadn't heard the interruption. "They found her body crumpled up behind one of the ladies toilets. The café had to close down for a while. The owner's son opened it up again about a year later."

"You seem to know a lot about this place."

"I like it here," she says, "I come every day after filming."

"You mean you don't get enough death during the day that you have to come here for more?"

"No," says Jess suddenly, banging her fists down on the table, "I don't. I don't get enough."

1974

You can't help but lie almost horizontal in these large armchairs covered with tie-dyed sheets that hide the cigarette burns and beer stains. You drum your fingers in time to the music and look up when the girls come in. They wave, you nod in their direction.

"Get us a beer, Shell," shouts Mike.

"Yeah, get us a beer, Shelly," echo the others.

She frowns, then smiles and joins the others at the bar. You can't help but watch as they stand lazily like heavy liquid slowly coming to rest in a curved glass. Carla, the prettiest, rests one foot on the metal rung of a barstool. They're all made up of fragments. Long legs stretching out from pleated mini skirts, long hair trailing down narrow backs. Long fingers, long nails filed to dangerous points, long earrings, long fake eyelashes. Short tempers.

You're bleary-eyed. You haven't been to school once in the last three weeks because you've been here every day, spending every evening in here till 2am, drinking coffee after coffee, tipping the waiter every other day till you're almost out of money. You were fired from the weekend job at the bike shop for not turning up and tonight you picked up the coins you spotted on your mother's dressing table. Shrapnel, nothing that will be missed. Not that you feel guilty anyway. And if you can talk the others into buying your drinks tonight, you will have that money for tomorrow. Because there is no doubt in your mind that you will be here tomorrow night and the night after that and the night after that. Your mother thinks you're doing drugs. She came right out and asked you. And you laughed and she became furious. But it was so funny. When you *had* been doing acid most weekends and getting stoned round at Mike's every other night, she hadn't thought anything of it. But now that you have a 'coffee habit' (or is it a café habit?) she assumes you're "putting all sorts of filthy things into your body."

The girls are back. They sit down noisily in the large settee on the other side of the table, a flash of white underwear and a quick tug of a skirt hem. A bottle of beer is placed in front of you.

"Stu's not drinking beer tonight. Are you, Stu? He's on the coffee," says Robert, "the hard stuff. So I'd better have his." He reaches over and slides it towards his other bottles, lining them up with a satisfied smile.

"What, you're not drinking? What's wrong with you? You don't smoke anymore, you don't drink. You've gone boring in your old age," says one of the girls, whose name you no longer care about. You stare instead at her leg, where a scar stretches from ankle bone to shin, a sheer white line that might have occurred in childhood and stretched with the growth of skin and bone.

"Are we leaving after these?" someone asks.

"Yeah, I want to catch the openers. About twenty minutes? You coming, Stu?"

105

"No," you say quietly. "I think I'll stay here."

1995

Saturday night in *Club Curieux* is busy. A waitress tries half-heartedly to sweep up crushed glass from beneath the stiletto-clad feet that won't or can't be still. Half-empty pint glasses rest on the cigarette machine, near the DJ box, on the tables that surround the dance floor. Natalie feels positively huge, surrounded by these stick-figures, squashed as she is into the uncomfortable wooden fold-away chair. She feels like her breasts are bulging against the fabric of her favourite top, her stomach pressing against the waistband of her jeans. There are four months to go yet. She will only get bigger, heavier, more sore, more fragile, more moody. Thinking that getting pregnant would change things, that Jamie would start coming home for his tea, and that perhaps the pregnancy would put an end to his fucking around

It was Jamie who had returned home from work early today with a bunch of flowers, who had pressed tender hands against her small rounded belly and suggested they go out for a change as they wouldn't have much chance when the baby was born. But when he had paused outside *Club Curieux* and then pushed open the door into the heat of mangled bodies, she had inwardly fumed. To bring her here, of all places. Here, where she had followed him that time, feeling like a film-spy, predator rather than prey; here where he had sat down at a table occupied by a red-haired woman, kissed her on the mouth, and guzzled down the beer that was already sitting on the table. Natalie hadn't known this place existed until that night. She had stood pasted to the window long enough to watch his big bloody foot play footsie with her ridiculously high heeled sandal; long enough to see her take hold of his hand and stroke the fingers whilst she talked at him. Her fingers had even played with his goddamn wedding ring. He had pulled away then and Natalie had thought perhaps he sensed the manipulative hand only a fucking mistress would deal. But it was simply to remove the ring and place it in the top pocket of his jacket.

As she watched she had known already that she was pregnant. She felt her life had taken on its own course. One over which she had no control. And now he has brought her to the same place and she feels the pull, again, the force of her life wanting to drag her in the opposite direction. Could she really go from loving him to hating him in such a short space of time?

Jamie says something to her across the table but she can't hear above the thud and echo of the music. She puts one hand behind her ear and shrugs.

"I said!" he shouts this time. "Are you okay? You look really pale!"

"I don't feel well" she says, looking around her. It is a half-truth. She just wants to get out of there, but there is no easy pathway to the front door. People are jammed in here like a tube train, all waiting to go somewhere. The building is hardly big enough to be utilized as a club, but it's the only place that stays open till late. During the day it's just a cosy café with a single table outside covered in wet leaves stuck to the red plastic, and two uncomfortable plastic chairs that were once white but which have never been cleaned of rain water. She wouldn't make it alive to the front door in this crowd. So she will choose the other route. She will go to the toilet, perhaps even find a back door the staff use to get out and away. Hopefully outside it's raining and she can wash away some of the grime.

"Where are the toilets?"

Jamie points to a door at the other end of the room.

"Okay. Get me a gin and tonic will you."

He nods and she scrapes the chair back and pushes her way through to the door, painted in swirls of green and pink. It opens onto a stone stairway that spirals down, each step narrowing to a point at the inner pillar. She makes her way down slowly, that much more afraid of falling since she found out about the baby. The awareness has made things that much more difficult. Everything she touches, everything she sees, everything she has always taken for granted, like crossing the road, like boiling a pan of water, like eating a cheese sandwich, have suddenly become rife with potential disaster. She is a careful girl. Never in her life has she suffered an accident more serious than a scraped knee but now she feels like some evil entity might stick out its evil leg and send her rolling down the stairs to a bloody, knotted death at the bottom. She knows how stupid it is. But still she holds onto that stone pillar for dear life, leaving sweaty handprints all the way down to the bottom.

She is met with three doors.

The ladies.

The gents.

And some other door, behind which she assumes the beer barrels are kept. But which, she crosses her fingers, might hold a way out. She turns the handle and presses her palm to the cold wood. The door opens onto inky blackness. But as it swings shut behind her, she catches a faint glimpse of metal and cries out loudly, a sound drowned out by the crescendo of music upstairs where Jamie waits, growing steadily more bored.

2016

They have been standing under the café awning for an hour. Right now there are just a handful of people in front and a trail of thirty or so behind, huddled under umbrellas. The trio ahead wear press badges and talk loudly about some show they went to last week. It's the opening night of the new art exhibition – 'Living Colour'. And it's Jake and Lilian's first date, though they've been friends for two years. Having spent the last few months giggling over their shared love of dark and nasty horror films and crime novels, they finally talked themselves (and each other) into going out together where he would pick her up at home and there would be the possibility of kissing and groping in a dark place. The cinema might have been the obvious location for such behaviour, but when Jake saw the poster for a new art show in *le Café Curieux*, it seemed like the perfect opportunity.

They've both been here before, many times. They've shared mocha milkshakes and plates of chips and discussed James Ellroy and David Lynch and Raymond Chandler. They've also discussed death over and over without coming up with anything more substantial than a queasy film-script. Lillian has pressed her fingertips against the many posters and plaques announcing the series of deaths that have happened right here in the café, including the suicides and naturals like heart attack and haemorrhage. It reads like a shopping list, or a list of British monarchs, or football scores. Jake has watched Lillian's fingers dance over the list, knowing her mind is reeling, trying to figure out some existential connection between them all.

The door opens and a man appears. "Okay, folks," he says. "Come on in."

The wooden tables with their graffiti-scratched surfaces have all gone. A small child sits at the piano and punches down hard on the keys. She sits on cushions piled up on the stool, and her feet don't reach the pedals, but that doesn't matter because it's obvious she can't play anyway. The sound is grating and important. In the centre of the room is the exhibit, cordoned off and surrounded with 'do not touch' signs. It will be difficult not to touch these. . . artefacts. Seated around two long rectangular dining tables are fifty people. At dinner. Each place is set with a plate, cutlery, a glass of what appears to be red wine. In the centre are salt and pepper shakers. In front of each plate is a small piece of card with a name scratched on in blue ink and shaky handwriting. There is food on the plates. Something black, something crushed like putty. It would appear to be made of plastic or wax, but on closer inspection (but not too close) the writhing maggots suggest the food is real and really rotting.

The diners are naked, but many are wearing watches, hats, shoes or they have the strap of a handbag slung lazily over a wrist, an unlit cigarette in the gash of a mouth where most of the teeth are gone, a badge whose pin strikes right through flesh, ripped stockings over broken legs. Most of these people are smiling. Those who do not have distinguishable faces still look happy enough; it's in their posture, their body language. The way they are holding up a glass to make a toast, the way they are patting their partner on the back, the way their glassy blue eyes sparkle.

With some of the diners their mode of death is not obvious. With others, it is obscenely apparent. There is Susanne Hughes, sitting at the head of the table, the oldest, the first, with a slit from clavicle to naval and her insides spilling. The girl beside her has wrists split to elbow and the man beside her, one Stuart Woolf, has a face so black and blue it looks like rotten fruit.

Jake squeezes Lillian's hand. Is this what she wanted? Is this the ultimate answer? Or is it just another question? She smiles at him and that is enough to tell him she is entertained at least.

Three people have walked out.

He circles his arms around her waist and they both stand motionless and take in the scene while the noises of (dis)approval rise from a revered whisper to a loud chatter in the accompanying fit-inducing flashes of magnesium.

It doesn't look very real, does it. - A question, spoken like a statement.

I wonder if the wigs are made of human hair.

I think it's positively grotesque. - But she doesn't walk away.

Look, that little boy is missing a finger.

Jake feels a wetness on his bare arm and realizes Lillian is crying. He puts his mouth to her ear, her soft hair, breathes into her – Is it her?

He knows it is. She is looking at a woman called Natalie Douglas, whose hips are wide and whose nipples are dark and who has a white scar on her belly from the removal of an appendix. She is holding a baby. It's a scrawny thing with skin that's red and wrinkled. It has tiny ears and a tiny bud of a nose and it sits foetal at five months, in the palms of her hands. Its own hand is pressed to the distended purplish breast and its face has been turned inward so the mouth sits neatly at the teat. But because of the odd angle of the head, the way it is pivoted on the short neck, it looks like it's been dropped from a height and landed like this, just off-centre. From here it is possible to see the hole where Natalie's left ear should be, and the caving-in of the skull around it.

Jake knows Lillian well enough now, he thinks, to know it is not the loss of life she sheds tears for.

"What is it, sweetheart?"

"I don't know. I don't know if I'm supposed to feel sad or sick or disgusted or. . . I don't know how I feel. It's new. It's overwhelming. I don't know how to explain. . ."

"You don't have to."

She turns to face him and he kisses her damp cheek, kisses her mouth.

"Are you ready to go on?"

She nods.

"Tell me."

"I'm ready, Jake."

He takes her hand in his and leads her around the edge of the exhibit, towards the door that they both know leads to the stairs. It is open but a curtain pulled across hides whatever is beyond. The café owner stands with arms crossed, in tuxedo and bow tie. He smiles as they come closer, the first, and pushes back the curtain just wide enough to let them pass. He collects their coins in the palm of his hand and draws the curtain behind them.

Reduction

Starting with the extremities, the furthest of the appendages, the fingertips that could crawl inside of me. The *only* way to be. To become. The tongue, the penis, inside they can be healed. The perimeters, the lines carved out. With my knife. The jutting ankle bone that heralds to my lips as I press them against. . . the Achilles heel, the weak spot, the place that might snap, like your wrists, or mine. With one fluid gesture, or one too many fast flicks in my direction. Your hips curved like a weapon, or the softest edge of a rose petal, the thorn, the stabbing motion inside my hand that weeps.

If your tongue were inside my mouth, would you try to speak? Or would you write your apologies in note form on the inside of my arm, where I never wash away the dirt? What are you? Do you wish you could eat me piece by piece like chocolate-covered spiders? I would squirm inside you, wriggle away so I couldn't be caught. I thought it was what I wanted but now I know I just want to scar you. My lover, my trophy, my other. My one. I don't know how many there are. If I cut you up would there be more of you? Or would you rejoin? If I can't see you how can I own you? If I can't consume you I will have to eat your words, cut them from your tongue, or from your hand. Or do they come straight from your heart? Mine come from my cunt and if I can't expel them I will swell to a size I can't handle. They will have to be cut out from the topside of my underbelly and I might bleed to death.

Come here, just put your fingers inside and let me look at your face, at the changing expressions, components. You're made up of many. I can separate the many from the few with one laceration. I can gut you like a fish. Then I could climb inside and draw hieroglyphs on your walls. Scar you on the silver side and before I retreat you can hold me close and reduce me to viscera. It's all conjecture anyway.

For more titles like this, please visit doghornpublishing.com.